I0610002

"Dollie", "Mollie"

Our own Heroes

Vol. I

"Dollie", "Mollie"

Our own Heroes
Vol. I

ISBN/EAN: 9783337193904

Printed in Europe, USA, Canada, Australia, Japan

Cover: Foto ©Andreas Hilbeck / pixelio.de

More available books at **www.hansebooks.com**

OUR

OWN HEROES.

A

THRILLING NARRATIVE.

BY "DOLLIE" AND "MOLLIE."

VOLUME I

ATLANTA, GA.:
OFFICE OF "THE SOLDIER'S FRIEND."

1863.

OUR OWN HEROES.

CHAPTER I.

A little cloud appears in the North East, the land of miasma and storms. At first it attracts little attention.— Gradually it attracts to itself other vaporous matter—it grows rapidly. The low, muttering thunder can be heard. Now the black flakes of cloud roll mountain high. The "forked tongued lightning" flashes athwart the angry heavens. The continent is shrouded in darkness. The "leaden hail stones" begin to fall. A thousand chieftains and a half million of heroes, as brave as ever drew a sword, rush to the rescue at the first tap of the drum.

We are to be "whipped into subjection" to the avaricious Puritan. The rights of sovereign States are no longer to be acknowledged. The galling chains of slavery were wrought for us by the most degraded would-be masters. The proud cavalier is to "tip his hat" to the haughty, persecuting, infidel Puritan, whose highest idea of liberty is to appropriate it *all* to himself, and persecute others. "Gain" is his God. "Ends, without any reference to means," is his motto. The making of "wooden nutmegs," "wooden canvassed hams," "paper-sole shoes," and the like, constitute his employment. Such are *some* of the

historic features of the people who, trampling the constitu
tion of the country under their feet, deluged the country
in blood.   To them must be attributed the guilt of the
present awful struggle.   They have murdered our brothers,
insulted our mothers and sisters, imprisoned our fathers,
desolated our fields, burnt our houses, and enveloped the
whole country in gloom.   To rescue our land from a worse
than Egyptian bondage, our noble youth, and many gray-
headed sires, formed themselves into "warrior bands."

Each State seemed to vie with her   sister States in her
efforts to meet and repel the invader.   "*You* must be our
Captain," "*You* must be our Lieutenant," were expressions
familiar to all.   "I am not competent," "Elect some one
else," were responses quite as common.   "Take him for an
officer who can lead us best," was the motto of our generous
and brave sons.

The stirring times found Albert B. and his gallant comrades in the hasty bivouac, where the "blue canopy was
their covering."   In the organization of the company Albert was unanimously chosen Captain; not because he
sought the place, nor because he was the intellectual superior of all the others; but as the office must be filled by
some one and he was competent to fill it, his comrades honored him with being their chief.   When he was declared
unanimously elected, he arose and spake as follows : "I feel
the compliment you have conferred upon me, fellow soldiers; but I can say in all sincerity, that I regret you have
made me your choice.   As I look around me, I see quite a
number of my brave comrades, who are, in my judgment,
more competent than myself to lead you.   But having
been chosen to lead you, I will do the best I can.   Humane and kind, I shall strive to inaugurate such discipline
as will contribute most to the efficiency, and intellectual
and moral good of those whom I have the honor to lead.
Please accept my thanks for your compliment, and rely

upon me as being ever ready to lead you to the bloody van, and to labor for your good in every particular."

There was one in this company whose name was not run for any office. His worth, as is often the case, was concealed under a reserved manner, and his real character could be known only by long and familiar acquaintance, or when some deed of noble daring was required. The name of this hero was Rufus V—

A few hastily collected blankets, and a small trunk, valise, or sachel, each, was all the bryyage our brave warriors took with them into the box cars into which they were crowded, as they left for ——, the city in which their regiment was to be formed. The tearful eyes of these brave warriors as they left the depot bespoke their tender sympathies for home—fathers, mothers, sisters, friends. Yet their manly bearing, their serious countenances, glowing with indignation at the wrongs offered their country, told to all who saw them, that in them the invaders would find warriors " worthy of their steel;" and that though the enemy might sweep over our country, it would not be until these valiant men were trampled under the feet of the despoiler.

All along the line of the railroad could be seen handkerchiefs waved from the hands of " maiden beauty;" while at every station flowers were showered upon them in the greatest profusion. As to the " substantials," as well as the " delicacies of life," they were brought by " lilly white" hands in great abundance, and gratuitously distributed among the soldiers.

On one occasion, when a beautiful young lady had brought a large basket of delicacies to them, one of the soldiers inquired the price. " *Price!*" said she. " Do you mean to insult me, sir ?"

" O no; certainly not. I did not suppose that you could afford to *give* away such nice cakes, especially since there are so many soldiers passing along this road."

" I hope," rejoined the young lady, "that I will never grow *so mean* as to sell provisions to those who are sacrificing everything for liberty. While my father has anything to eat, a hungry soldier shall never be permitted to pass our house without something."

Saying this she handed the basket into the car, blushing deeply as her dark eyes fell upon our hero, V—.

After many expressions of gratitude to the fair donor, the basket was handed back to her and she handed it to a nice servant girl, who had brought the basket to the depot. The maiden blushingly stepped back a few paces, and gave an occasional glance through the cars, apparently with no other object than to give a look of approbation upon the brave defenders of her home, but really to see him who had caused such strange and unbidden feelings to rise in her heart. Her confusion, however, did not pass unobserved ; for the strong arm that lifted the burdened basket into the car, had noted her peculiar "rosy blush." Others, too, had observed the same thing, as also a similar confusion in the noble Rufus.

The beauty, simplicity, and grace, coupled with the undoubted patriotism of the maiden, prevented the men from saying anything to confuse either Rufus or the fair stranger. Besides, there was something so attractive, so bewitching in her manners, as to throw a " kind of spell" over all who saw her. Presently the engine whistled, the cars started, and a shout of " God bless you," with waiving of handkerchiefs, parted the strangers.

The maiden left, straightway, for home, lest she should betray the feelings of her heart. She went away wondering who the soldier could be. " Who can this be ? What a complete simpleton I was, to blush so in the presence of strangers ! And why should I have experienced this indescribable feeling when I looked into the face of that stranger ?" were questions which arose in her mind as she hastened home.

The cars had not gone far when "you are born for luck," fell from several lips at the same time. "Why, Rufus, how is it that you blushed so deeply when those beautiful black eyes met yours? There is *danger* ahead for you young man."

"Yes," shouted another, "there is danger 'ahead' and danger *behind!*"

"You cannot blame one for admiring beauty," said Rufus, striving to conceal his evident confusion.

"No, of course not," replied a comrade; "but if I am not very much mistaken, you are guilty of doing a little more than simply *admiring* her beauty!"

"I should never think the less of you," said the Captain, "if you were really to love so beautiful and graceful a lady. I give it as my opinion that she is worthy of any man's love."

Thus the time passed away, as they neared the city, where the next day a regiment was to be formed.

"I suppose," said one of the company, "that we will have to elect a Colonel and other officers to-morrow; shall we all vote for you for Colonel?"

"If you think I am competent to fill the office, and wish to get rid of me as captain, you may vote for me."

"I have no doubt as to your competency, but I am sure none of us wish to get rid of you. You have destroyed your vote with us this time. I shall vote for some one else."

They soon reached the depot, took out their baggage, and slept under the car-shed till day. Their sore hips reminded them when they arose in the morning, of the truth of the poem, "There's *no place* like home."

The election of field officers came off, and though there was much intriguing for office—disgraceful barterings for votes—Captain B——, who did not dream of promotion, was elected Colonel, contrary to the general rule in such cases. The political tricksters, who thought more of their own promotion than of their bleeding country, (whose interest, in days of peace, they had sacrificed on the altar of their unholy ambition,) felt no little disappointment at their defeat. Already they had selected, each, his "staff officers"—men, whose principles were akin to their own.—These would-be officers felt no little disappointment at the result of the election. They had pictured to themselves "easy" as well as *profitable* "berths."

The Colonel elect made a short, sensible speech to his regiment, thanking them for the honor they had conferred on him, and assuring them that, to the best of his ability, he would do his *whole* duty. The disappointed aspirants thought the speech a "tame thing," whispered privately that the "regiment was disgraced by having such an officer," and murmured their "unwillingness to serve under him." The sensible, honest portion of the men were delighted at the prospect of having a good and brave officer.

Captain B——, now Colonel, having been promoted, Lieutenant James M—— became Captain. His character you may infer, when I tell you that "his heart was kind," "his intellect refined," "his conduct exemplary," and "his words chaste."

It may be proper to state that Mr. John R—— was elected Lieutenant Colonel, and Joseph I—— Major.

As might have been expected, the Colonel appointed a devotedly pious and intellectual minister Chaplain.

The character of these officers the reader will be able to appreciate from what will be said of them hereafter.

No sooner had the Colonel entered regularly upon his duties, than it was observed that no ordinary man was in command. It soon became apparent, also, that none of those low vices, such as gambling, drinking, swearing, and other kindred evils, would be tolerated. This impression was first made on the regiment by the following circumstance: A Lieutenant, vexed because one of his men did not exactly please him, cursed and abused him at an awful rate. The Colonel hearing him, sent for him to report at his head-quarters. Taking his sword from him, and giving him his only scat—"a camp-stool," the Colonel addressed him as follows:

"Did I hear you cursing one of your men?"

The confused Lieutenant replied: "Yes sir; he acted very badly, and—"

"That will do, sir. You confess your own guilt. Now, sir, did you know that you have committed a two-fold crime?"

"What are they?"

First, you used profane language, which the 'army regulations,' as well as the Word of God, positively forbids.— [See Army Regulations, and the Bible.]

"Your second crime consists in cursing and abusing one of your men. You have *no* right to do this; nor will it be tolerated in this regiment."

"But he provoked me, Colonel."

"*Provoked you!* Suppose he did; is that any reason why *you* should commit such an outrage? Does *his* wrong —admitting that he committed it—justify your wrong?"

"Well," said the Lieutenant, anxious to be relieved from his troubles, "what is the penalty?"

"You must pay—how many oaths did you use?"

"I do not remember."

Upon questioning others, it was agreed that he had used not less than five oaths.

"Having sworn five oaths, you must pay five dollars."

"But," inquired the astonished officer, "is there any *law* for this exaction?"

The Colonel thereupon opened the Army Regulations, and read the following: "Any non-commissioned officer or soldier who shall use any profane oath or execration, shall incur the penalties expressed in the foregoing article [16¾ cents for each oath, &c.]; and a commissioned officer shall forfeit and pay, for each and every such offence, one dollar."

"But" said the Lieutenant, who knew for the first time that there was any such law, and wishing to come off as lightly as possible, "may not the whole be considered as one *swearing scrape?*"

The proof is very plain against you; you used five oaths, and must pay five dollars."

The mortified Lieutenant "footed the bill," and inquired how the other offence might be attoned for; to which the Colonel replied:

"I will be satisfied, so far as I am concerned, if you will make a snitable apology to the abused private."

"This demand is much worse than the other," replied the Lieutenant.

"But, if you prefer it," answered the Colonel, "you can stand your chance at a court-martial."

"Call the private, and make him apologize for his wrong, and I will readily do the same."

"No, sir; your wrong rests upon its own basis, and you must account for it accordingly. No misconduct on his part, can justify your treatment of him. After your case is disposed of, we will look into his."

The young officer hesitated.

"Do you prefer a court-martial? Then a court-martial you shall have."

The alternative was a bitter one; but the officer, dreading the consequences of a trial by a court-martial, at last consented to make the required apology; which he did like a man.

The private was then called to the Colonel's tent, where the following conversation ensued:

"How did you offend your officer?"

"I did not obey his orders."

"What were his orders?"

"To bring some wood and make him a fire. I would

have obeyed the order, if it had been given in a mild way."

"The case is a very plain one," said the Colonel, "and I therefore dismiss you at once. No officer of his rank has the right to make any such demands.

The Colonel, thinking this a good opportunity for impressing his men with a few important lessons, summoned the regiment together, and addressed them thus:

"Fellow-soldiers, we have enlisted in a great cause—the cause of liberty. · Our country is threatened with invasion; our churches with desecration; our homes with flames. To prevent these dire results, we have forsaken home, friends, and comfort, and will march soon to meet the foe on the battle-field. We all have a common interest and a common destiny; and should, therefore, be a band of brothers.

"Officers should understand their duties—how to drill and manœuvre their men—in a word, they should understand 'military tactics' thoroughly. They should understand *how* far their authority extends over their men, and *where* their authority ceases. And more, they should be firm, generous, kind and gentlemanly towards their men, exacting no more than what is right, nor accepting less from their men. You should remember that the men whom you command are your equals in everything except in office.

"You, who are privates, have to bear the heaviest burdens of war. You must submit to wholesome discipline. There is nothing degrading in this; nor will any honorable-minded private feel humiliated at this. You must learn to be ruled, or rather to rule yourselves by submitting to the laws necessary for the regulation of an army. To desire less than this, is to desire the devastation of our country, the destruction of our homes, and the loss of our liberties.

"To be good privates will entitle you to greater honors than if you were officers, since those who sacrifice most in a good cause deserve most praise.

"To officers and privates I wish to say, once for always, that the 'army regulations' shall be strictly carried out. No profanity will be allowed; drunkenness will be punished in the most summary way; and every vice shall receive its merited rebuke or punishment at my hands.

"Let us, one and all, see to it that we *honor* our positions, and our country will honor us."

Saying this, he dismissed them.

This address made a decided impression on the minds of all. Some were delighted—others were mad. The virtuous rejoiced, the vicious were alarmed and disappointed. They saw that their expectation of "fun" was "nipped in the bud."

The few days that they remained in the city were spent in getting up their camp equipments, and in "drilling." It was wonderful to see how much the young Colonel knew about "tactics." He seemed to "know it all" from the very first, though he had never read a book on the subject until he entered the service. The most casual observer could not fail to see the rapid improvement made in drill. All the officers seemed to vie with their peers in seeing who could understand his duties and execute them best. A similar spirit pervaded the ranks. With such material it was an easy matter to have a model regiment, and such this was. The most perfect discipline and drill, as well as the best moral deportment, were the things which our noble Colonel aimed at. The men, most of them, at least, caught his spirit, and fell in with his way of thinking and acting.

It is wonderful, how much influence one mind has over another! An officer, especially, has, from his position, ready access to the minds of his men, and very soon impresses himself on those whom he governs. If he is a noble type of man he will elevate his men and gradually assimilate them to himself; and if he is a vicious character, he will find many in a regiment, whom he can very soon degrade to his own level. It is to be regretted that assimilation takes place more readily when the example is vicious than when it is virtuous. This can be accounted for only by reference to the fact that men are naturally more inclined to vice than to virtue—more in love with sin than with holiness.·

"Off to the cars, boys—quick, or we'll be too late," said the Colonel as he snatched his valise and hastened towards the depot. An order had been received requiring the regiment to hasten to ——, where it was expected an attack would be made at an early day.

"Glad," said private V—, to himself, "that we are going in this direction. Who knows that I will not get a glimpse of that form that called into exercise those strangely pleasant emotions that I experienced a few days ago!"

The cars rattled, and the boys generally appeared to be in a great glee; but V— thought of little else but her whose image had been indellibly impressed upon his mind. Her graceful form and beautiful features were ever present with him, and her "rosy blush" bloomed fresh in his imagination, while a "crimson glow" flushed his manly cheeks.

"What would I not give for just one glance at the graceful beauty!" silently sighed the hero, as they approached near the station where he had seen her before. "But I must move my seat, for should I see her, these rude boys would desecrate my holy affections by offensive laughing and jesting."

Accordingly he changed seats, getting in the corner of the car near a hole that had been made by breaking off the plank. Of course our hero did not do this himself; but he regarded it as quite a convenience to himself on this occasion.

The cars stopped, but no maiden could he see. The train ran an irregular schedule, which accounts for the absence of many citizens—ladies and gentlemen.

"·Sad, sad, indeed," exclaimed V—, with a deep sigh, which on an occasion less jolly than the present, would certainly have attracted the attention of his comrades.

The cars began to move off, and still she did not come. His feelings no one could appreciate, who had entertained naught but emotions less pure. He would have sacrificed anything but his country, his honor and his religion, for one single glimpse of her, to him, angelic form. The "iron horse" had run about half a mile, when, still gazing out, he saw a stately mansion on a beautiful eminence about one hundred yards from the road. The nicely arranged flower yard bespoke the elegance of the family that resided there.

"What strange form is that in that rose-decked bower! Can it be—it is the identical!"

As the cars came opposite the bower, she came out, and seeing that the train was laden with soldiers, she waved them a hearty welcome; but did not recognize him who had extracted from her heart, its first and purest admiration. *Virtus* (for this was our heroe's name,) had a good look, and never mortal enjoyed a vision more. Well for him that he was in a dark corner of the car; for otherwise he would have exposed a secret which was as dear to him as his honor.

Whizzing they went by, and the precious sight was violently intercepted by the rude excavation through which the cars passed.

"One point is made," thought Virtus, when he had recovered himself from the delightful shock. "I *know where she lives*. And if the fortunes of war ever permit it, I intend to see her again." Embalming the "sacred form" afresh in his affections, he went back to his former seat, and participated in the conversation of his comrades, as if nothing had happened.

Time passed off pleasantly, until at 3 o'clock, A. M., they were ordered to collect their baggage, and get out of the cars. The order is promptly obeyed, they kindle hasty fires, spread down their blankets, and gently yield to "nature's sweet restorer."

At early dawn reveille is beaten, and the weary soldiers, who, in former days were wont to consult their pleasure about getting up, spring to their feet, and to a man, answer to their names at roll-call. And now hands unaccustomed to drudgery were seen working up dough. Breakfast over, the Colonel, who had appointed an Adjutant pro tem., summoned Virtus to his head-quarters. "I have sent for you," said the Colonel, " to tender you the adjutant's office. I hope you will accept it."

"Thank you, Colonel, for the compliment; but you must allow me to assure you, sir, that I cannot accept the office which you have so generously tendered me."

"Why?"

"Simply because I have vowed to live through the war, or until I fall on the battle-field, a private."

"Are you opposed to being an officer on principle, or is it because I am Colonel of the regiment?" inquired the astonished officer.

"On principle, sir," he replied. "I will add, too, that there is no man in the Confederacy under whom I would sooner serve than under yourself."

"Let us now," said the Colonel, "investigate the 'principle' on which your objections are founded; and if this can be removed, I feel assured that you will yield, and accept the office."

"I am ready for the investigation, and will, of course, 'yield,' if my objections are not well founded."

"It devolves upon you to establish the validity of your objections. You may proceed."

"Very well, sir; I will give my reasons in order. 1st. According to your own speech the other day, I would sacrifice, by becoming an officer, a portion of the honor which I hope to receive.

" 2d. The country demands the service, as privates, of as good men as she has.   While I do not claim that I am one of the *best*, I feel that I can make a *good* private.

" 3d. The position of the private requires him to make the greatest sacrifice for his country's independence, and I am unwilling that any one should sacrifice more for this object than myself.   And

" 4th. The private's position is much more favorable to his moral development than is an officer's."

The Colonel, after listening with great admiration to the reasons of his friend, replied : " Your first reason is one to which I cannot reply, without abandoning the principle assumed in my address to which you allude.   Your second reason is quite as unanswerable.   The third, while nearly akin to the first, furnishes the highest evidence of a pure patriotism, which I can but admire.   But the fourth requires some proof.   Will you elaborate the reason, if you please ; for if *my* position is more unfavorable to morality and religion, I think I shall resign."

" I will grant your request, Colonel, if you insist upon it ; but I would prefer, for two reasons that you would withdraw the request."

" What are those reasons ?"

" 1st. My three reasons, whose validity you have conceded, are sufficient to justify my course ; and 2d. I fear that you might be induced to resign your position, which I would regard as a great calamity."

" If there be any truth in your fourth reason, you as a man of moral integrity, are bound to give me all the light in your possession.   If my *morals* are to be more endangered by being an officer than by being a private, I would resign my position, if I were commander-in-chief."

" As you insist upon it, I will give my thoughts freely : It cannot be denied that adversity and self-denial *tend* to promote humility, patience and meekness, which are virtues of rare worth ; and on the other hand, it is equally evident to my mind that prosperity *tends* to foster pride, and stimulate its kindred elements.

"There can be no question in my mind as to the moral tendency of offices on those who fill them—it must be for evil. Yet, if an officer has perfect knowledge of his own character, and perfect control of his feelings, he may be able to arrest this evil tendency, and improve in moral worth. But I am thoroughly convinced that I do not possess such knowledge; and, if I did, that I would not be able to control all my feelings."

"Come in Major, and take a seat," said the Colonel as the former politely gave the latter a "military salute."

The Colonel, looking at his watch, found that he had already postponed too long, an order to cook "three day's rations." The order must not be postponed a moment longer, for at 12 o'clock, M., they must leave for the "mountain pass," whither two regiments had already gone to prevent the enemy, who were about 10,000 strong, from passing through The order was given, and the soldiers, wondering where they would be ordered, began to cook their "hasty rations,"

Virtus, supposing that the Major might have private business with the Colonel, and wishing to have his rations ready in time, arose, excused himself, and departed.

"We will talk of these matters again soon," said the Colonel, addressing himself to Virtus.

"Very well, sir; but you must not do what you proposed."

"We will see about that," said the other.

"About what?" inquired the Major.

"About some private matters, sir," answered the Colonel, who would have been glad the whole regiment, and even the whole army, were acquainted with the *reasons* of the young hero, who had just left his tent; but he felt that the logic of Virtus was too pure, his patriotism too refined, and his moral philosophy too elevated to be appreciated by

2

many men. So he did not, from his limited acquaintance
with the Major, feel at liberty to disclose them to him even.

The Major saw in an instant the impropriety of his question, and asked pardon, which was readily granted.

The Major remained but a short time, when he retired,
leaving the Colonel to his own meditations. "What a
remarkable man I have found in this private! What
intelligence, what logic, what philosophy! I cannot
answer his arguments. What shall I do? I have, as it
appears to me, committed myself to him in such a way as
to make it necessary for me to resign."

Such thoughts occupied his mind until the mail boy
came in, handing him an official document. "What can
this mean?" queried the Colonel, as he opened the envelope.
"A Brigadier General, indeed! Who ever *thought* of such
a thing!!"

He was one of those modest men, who naturally shrank
from office, and who knew a thousand men that would, in
his judgment, fill the office much better than himself

To the official document was appended an order that, if
he should accept the appointment he must take command
of all the regiments at —— Gap. He knew not what to
do. "I know nothing," said he to himself, "about the
duties of a Brigadier, and I have only three days in which
to prepare myself for this important and highly responsible
office. I have a mind to write the authorities at once, declining the position."

"Looking at his watch again, he found that he did not
have time to write—the moment of their departure was at
hand. He sent out orders to all the companies to get
ready as soon as possible, for their long march of about 40
miles.

Having imbibed, partially at least, the spirit and prompt-
ness of their leader, the men were ready to march within a
few moments.,

"Forward, march!" echoed along the line from one who

was destined to be a world-renowned leader. "Forward" they went, moving in "veteran style." Moving on at the head of the column, the unassuming leader, looked the complete General—*one of nature's own making; for Generals, like " Poets, are born, not made."* Casting his eyes backwards along the lines, he saw the manly form of Virtus, somewhat bent under the heavy burden that he was bearing. "There," thought he, "is one of nature's noblemen—a man better, far better prepared to be a Brigadier than myself; and yet he proudly scorns office! I would prefer being just such a man as he is, than to be Lieut. General. What a noble soul !"

Coming to a beautiful shade and one of those "crystal fountains" that show how the God of nature sometimes lavishes his blessings on an unworthy populace—even upon *tories*—the Colonel ordered his men to halt, get water, and rest. They sipped the perennial fount with a relish known only to soldiers. While they were resting the Colonel took occasion to summon Virtus to him, and insisted that he should relieve him of his burden. "If you will not allow me to carry all, let me have at least a part of your baggage."

" Thank you, Colonel, for your great kindness; yet you must allow me to carry my own baggage. You would not lessen my honor by relieving me of my burden ?"

" It is remarkable, sir, that you will not allow me to do anything for you !"

" You cannot carry every soldier's baggage, Colonel; and if you should single me out from the whole regiment, it might subject you to the charge of partiality, and me to the envy of some of my comrades."

The argument was so complete that the Colonel, smiling, went away and ordered the regiment to "shoulder arms." This done, the Colonel notified his men in a short address that there were many tories in the country through which they had to march; that often "bushwhackers" would fire

upon them from behind trees and from mountain tops; that
there should be no "straggling" &c. The line of march
was resumed, and they went with little interruption till
night. They pitched their tents in a beautiful cove between
two spurs of the mountain, near a large creek, whose
bounding waters sung a sweet "lullaby," gently inviting
sleep to the weary soldier.

Supper over, and the pickets having been posted all
around, the Colonel sent for Virtus to visit his head-
quarters; and felt no little regret on learning that he was
"out on picket."

Now must be related an incident that mars the meagre
comforts of "camp life," and makes the moralist shudder
at the consequences of war. Night had but just thrown
her sombre mantle over the face of earth, when a dark
plan is concocted, and a black deed is executed! A number
of soldiers, led by a Lieutenant, left the encampment and
went to a house near by, for the purpose of getting a
warm supper and a "supply of eatables" to last them
several days. There was no wrong in this of itself; but
stealing off, and especially the design of supplying their
wants (which were more imaginary than real,) without paying anything, were crimes which a life-time of after recti-
tude could never atone for.

Entering the house, they found an old lady with her two
daughters and a little son, sitting by the fire.

"We wish supper!" peremptorily demanded the Lieutenant.

"We are over with supper, gentlemen, and it will be no
little trouble for me to go and cook it now."

"It matters not about the 'trouble,' madam, we must
have supper."

"I hope, gentlemen, you do not intend to insult defence-
less women!"

"We must have supper, madam," was the stern and un-
feeling reply.

"Well, sir, if you *must*, I suppose you will have no objection to cooking it," answered the old lady.

Upon this, the soldiers grew very angry, and began to curse and swear at a terrible rate. "You are a miserable set of *tories*, and you cannot claim protection at our hands."

"Tories!" exclaimed the old woman; "there was never a better Southern man than my husband, who is now in the army with two sons."

"That's all stuff!" replied the soldiers. "You wish merely to save your property by this trick."

Upon this they went into the dining room, and began to search for something to eat. Finding little, they went to the smoke-house, battered down the door, and went in to help themselves. Coming out, some of them went to the the chicken-house, and began to lay in a supply of poultry.

Meantime the little boy had stolen out of the house unobserved, and found his way to the Colonel's headquarters. Immediately on relating his story, the Colonel ordered a dozen soldiers, under Capt. ——, to hasten to the scene of oppression, and bring the depredators to his head-quarters. Within a few minutes the squad were off, and soon drew near the house. Chickens were squalling, the thieves cursing, and the old woman was trying to shame the scoundrels. Ascertaining the number engaged in this foul crime, the squad rushed suddenly upon them, arresting all but one, who made his escape through the backyard. The pitiful cowards who were brave in a contest with helpless women, crouched before the gallant and indignant soldiers who were sent to arrest them. The Captain made them carry the meat back, turn the chickens loose, and set out for the Colonel's tent. They had not gone far when the Lieutenant proposed to the Captain that he should release them all, and added the promise that they would never act so any more.

"Too late, gentlemen, you must 'face the music!'" retorted the indignant officer.

" I will give you $1,000 if you will release us."

" Money cannot purchase your release. But you miserable wretch, do you suppose that I can be bribed ?"

Finding that it was useless to attempt to bribe him, they submitted to be driven on into the Colonel's presence. These gentry were put under a strong guard, and ordered to await their trial by court-martial. It is needless to say that the extreme of the law was visited upon the heads of these wretches.

It was about mid-night when the pickets fired their guns, and such of them as had escaped death or captivity, came running into camp.

" What now, boys," exclaimed the Colonel, as they ran in.

" The enemy are upon us—they fired a full volley among us before we were aware of their presence !" answered the officer in command of the pickets.

Within a few minutes the regiment was arranged in "battle line," and awaited the advance of the enemy. But no enemy approached. At length a few companies were sent to the scene of the recent firing, to see if they could make any discovery of the assailants. Two of our men were found dead, and three were seriously wounded.

" Easy," said the Colonel, (for he was among the foremost,) " I hear them now—they are retreating over the top of that mountain."

Remaining quiet until he was convinced that the enemy had fled away, the wounded and dead were cared for. Not seeing Virtus among the pickets who ran in, the Colonel feared that he was among the killed or wounded, and the manner in which he examined the unfortunate five, showed how tenderly he regarded his men and how high an estimate he placed upon Virtus, especially. But our hero was not among the number. "Where is private Virtus?" earnestly enquired the Colonel.

" I recollect distinctly," said the picket officer, " seeing him after the order to retreat, was given. He was standing boldly in the van loading his gun."

" Why did you not order him to retreat along with you ?" asked the Colonel.

" The general order to ' retreat,' was given, and I took it for granted that as all the others heard the order, he must have heard it too."

" He must be captured," replied the Colonel, sighing deeply.

Leaving two full companies as pickets, the Colonel with the others returned to camps—the latter to sleep, the former to lament the sad fortune of his loved friend.

The attacking party was nothing more than a company of " bushwhackers," who waylay the roads for the purpose of killing and robbing. The Colonel inferring the direction of their camp from the noise which they made in their retreat, determined to make an effort to dislodge them, and recapture his friend. Here arose a serious question of duty. He had received orders to be at the —— Gap at such a time, in anticipation of an early attack. "If I stop to hunt up these robbers, I may be behind time ; but how can I lose so valuable a friend without an effort to rescue him?" were thoughts that troubled him.

Making a nice estimate of the distance to the Gap, and finding that, by a " forced march," he could spare half a day, he resolved to spend this time in searching for Virtus. Accordingly he went to Capt. M—, who was on picket, and laid his plans before him. The Captain, who was a great friend and admirer of Virtus, was ready to lend any assistance in his power to rescue him from the grasp of such an ignoble foe. He, accordingly, proposed to take his company and move silently to the mountain's top, to see if he could make any discovery of the enemy, and report as soon as possible. This was agreed to and Capt. M—, with his gallant company, began to ascend the craggy

heights of the mountain.   On reaching the summit he
found that there was a deep ravine winding along between
the mountains on his right.   No light, save the " celestial
stellas," was anywhere visible.   The " hooting " of the
owl, and the roaring of the small waterfall, were the only
sounds audible.

Moving forward, as quietly as possible for about a half a
mile, they again halted, to look and listen.   No discovery
being made, they moved on still farther, nearly about the
same distance, when a light, reflected from a deep ravine
upon the opposite mountain, was clearly visible.   Advancing nearer they could hear indistinct sounds of the human
voice.

" We have found their nest," said the Captain in a low
whisper.   " Let us return as silently as we came, and report our success."

Off they went, at a more rapid pace than they had advanced to the point of discovery ; and soon halted in the
presence of the Colonel.   " A complete success " was reported, and the Colonel ascertaining that the bushwhackers
did not number more than probably one hundred, quickly
called for four companies, to go with him in order to make
" clean work of the whole establishment." The companies
were divided into two parties of two companies each ; one
taking the rout of the company that had located the enemy,
and the other ascending by a circuitous path the mountain
on the other side of the ravine—it being the purpose of
the Colonel to surround and capture the whole party.
The Colonel commanded one party and Captain M— the
other.   It was the agreement that they should surround the
tory camp before light, and be ready, at a signal, to dash
upon them at early light.   The parties gained their respec-
tive positions just before the nightingale sent forth his
first melodious note.   It soon became evident to both com-
manders that it was impossible to reach the enemy, owing
to the perpendicular mountain sides that lay between them.

What could they do? cut off from each other, and subject, each, to be attacked very soon by they did not know how many. Should they remain on the mountain tops the enemy would find little trouble in escaping up the ravine. And if there was any way of getting to the bottom of the ravine so as to intercept their retreat, it had not yet been discovered.

A courier was at once dispatched to camps with orders to the Lieut. Colonel to take three companies and advance up the ravine , having the courier as a guide.

This done, the Colonel passed up higher, in search of a place to descend the precipice, and Capt. M— luckily did the same thing. They travelled probably half a mile above the tory camp before they found the least prospect of a descent. As they advanced they found that the mountain sides began to recede gradually from a perpendicular, which led to the hope that soon they would be able to descend to the bottom. In this they were not disappointed; for soon they found that, by holding to the bushes, they could make some headway to the bottom of the dark pit far below them. The " streaks of light" were now beginning to fall on the tree tops, which seemed but to intensify the darkness into which they were plunging.

After much difficulty in falling over rocks and cliffs, the Colonel with his band came near the bottom of the gulf, when all of a sudden, he heard a low muttering on the opposite side. " Can this be the enemy?" he inquired easily. " If so, we may get into trouble. But these suppressed voices that I hear, cannot come from the enemy, unless he has discovered our movements and is making his escape."

Silently he moved on to the waters edge and was halted by a soldier in Capt. M—'s command. They soon recognized, to their mutual gratification, that they were friends. Though it was now day on the mountain tops, it was night where these heroes were standing. It was a serious question with them, how they should make their way down the ravine. Slowly they began to feel their way over the precipitous rocks, that would have effectually blocked up the path of men less determined. But by climbing upon and sliding down the high rocks, they made about a quarter of a mile per hour. They were now within 400 yards of the encampment, when several difficulties arose in the Colonel's mind. If they should fire upon the encampment, they might kill Virtus; if they should not fire, there was great danger of losing more of his own men than if they should commence the attack vigorously. He determined, therefore, to wait until it became light enough to distinguish friend from foe. This would give ample time for the Lieut. Colonel to bring up his men below. It was about light enough to distinguish a man, when a half a mile or more below, two muskets were fired, and then a volley echoed up the deep ravine Presently nearer by, an alarm was given, and a hasty retreat ordered. Soon it became apparent that the tories were making up the ravine.

"Now," said the Colonel, "we've got them—don't fire without orders; and be sure then, that you do not shoot a friend."

On came the stampeders, pitching hastily over the rocks, until at last, to their great astonishment, they found that they were completely hemmed in. The Colonel's four companies all arising from their ambush, seemed to the tories to be a legion. They were promptly ordered to surrender, which they were quite willing to do. There were about 60 of these poor deluded wretches who surrendered.

The Colonel now advanced toward their camps, and about the time he got in full view of them, the force from below came up. A friendly recognition soon took place between the Colonel and Lieut. Colonel, and soon they congratulated each other on their signal and bloodless triumph. But only a *part* of their victory had been achieved, which to the Colonel would have appeared almost fruitless without the rescue of Virtus.

"W ere," inquired the Colonel of the tory Captain, " is the prisoner you captured from us a few hours ago ?"

The Captain hesitated.

"You must tell instantly, or your life will pay the forfeit."

On seeing the determination of the Colonel, the miserable tory turned his eyes towards the base of the mountain, and said, " He is yonder, sir."

" Go with me, and let us see where he is."

On approaching, the mouth of a small cave appeared.

" He is in there, sir."

" Alive or dead ?"

" Alive, sir ; but he cannot speak."

" Why not ?"

" He is gagged, sir, to prevent his making any noise."

" Is he bound ?"

" Yes, sir, to avoid the necessity of guarding him."

" Bring a light," cried the Colonel.

A light was quickly brought, and on looking in, they saw several forms all bound. Looking about he soon discovered Virtus, who was certainly willing that the Colonel should " lighten his burden of war " for once. It is impossible to describe their joy at this meeting. The Colonel advanced to him and loosed his fetters and his tongue as soon as possible. The warmest gratitude of Virtus was expressed to the Colonel for his recovery from this miserable dungeon.

The other prisoners were also released. Some of them were picked up as " stragglers " a few weeks before ; others had been cruelly seized at the dark hours of night, and dragged from their homes because of their Southern sentiments.

Turning to the Captain of this robber band, the Colonel inquired : " What do you do with your prisoners ?"

" We release them, sir, after keeping them a few days."

The manner of the robber led the Colonel to believe that prisoners captured by this band were very probably killed. But having no positive proof of the fact, he sent the prisoners to the rail road under a strong guard.

At 9 o'clock A. M. he renewed his march towards the Gap, which he reached the next day evening.

The regiments at the Gap had been expecting an attack from a strong Abolition force, but as yet " the ball had not opened."

" What shall I do ?" was the question of vital moment with the Colonel at this time. " Shall I accept the position of Brigadier General, or shall I resign even my Coloneley, and go, where the argument seems to lead me, to the ranks ?"

At this juncture he sent for private Virtus. (For though their stations were very different, yet he felt that if there was any difference between himself and Virtus in an intellectual and moral point of view, that difference was in favor of the private.)

He knew that Virtus was a young man of great purity of character and force of intellect ; and he naturally loved to hear him talk. Besides, he was sure he could make a strong point with him, as he had been offered a Brigadier Generalship and would gladly make Virtus his " A. A. G."

Virtus makes his appearance in front of the Colonel's tent.

" Good evening ! Come in ! How do you feel since you got out of the clutches of the robbers ?"

" Very comfortable, as well as grateful, I assure you."

" In the pressure of business, I omitted to ask how you came to be captured."

" I heard no order to retreat—and I could not afford to leave without orders"

" But did you not see the others run ?"

" Yes, and rather too soon, as I thought. If all had

remained at their posts, I have no doubt that the enemy would have retired after a second volley. But when they saw our pickets run so soon, they rushed forward and came upon me almost unawares."

"Well," said the Colonel, "this is all over now, and I hope you will never be so unfortunate again. I have received a Brigadier's appointment, requiring me to take charge of all the troops at this place. Now, should I accept the appointment, I wish to know whether you will accept an Adjutant General's position, having the rank of Captain?"

"My arguments, my much esteemed sir, are just the same in this case as they were in the former. The change from a Lieutenancy to a Captaincy does, in no wise, change great principles. I know that it would be very agreeable to human nature to wear ' three bars,' ride a fine horse, and live in ' refined society,' yet I regard my moral welfare as of first importance to me."

"Suppose I should tell you that I will not accept the position offered me, unless you will be my Adjutant?"

"I will be sorry of it, but I cannot help it, Colonel. My course is fixed. I have determined to serve my country as a private."

"What, then, would you advise 'me to do?"

"You must act for yourself, sir—the responsibility is yours. It will, however, afford me much pleasure to have you as my General."

"Your elevated decisions, I very much admire. Would that I could have the same determined purpose that rules your action. You, I feel assured, are even more competent than myself to fill any military office; and yet you proudly spurn promotion."

"Thank you for the compliment, Colonel. I hope I shall always have your respect and confidence.

"We need men of integrity to lead our forces; otherwise we cannot hope for success. Moreover, if immoral, drunken officers are to have our armies in their hands, we cannot expect them to exert any but a bad influence on our soldiers. You should consider this subject well before you decide against holding office."

"But does not this argument do away with your own position? If good men are needed to fill offices—and I grant that they are—may it not become the *duty* of such men to accept office when it is tendered them? On this plea, I know of no man more competent to fill the position offered you than yourself. Come, waive your scruples, and accept."

"There is much truth, Colonel, in what you say; yet the arguments previously given you, are to my mind, perfectly conclusive. If they are, I do not feel at liberty to set them aside. Moreover, I am a peculiar person. I have to war constantly against pride. If I should become an officer I know that my wicked heart would soon become puffed up; and once I recede from my position, especially when my arguments are not answered, I would easily be led off from that meekness and humility which I deem so necessary to soul prosperity."

"I perceive, sir, that you are not to be moved from your position, unless I first remove your arguments, and this, I confess, I am not able to do.

"I will assume command here, because I think my duty requires me to do so; and whenever your notions change, I will try to make a place for you on my staff."

"I hope, sir, that I am actuated by something higher than a mere ' *notion* '—I have *arguments* upon which to stand, and if you or any one else will show them to be false, I will abandon them."

"I did not design, my dear sir, to wound your feelings in the slightest. I very much admire both your arguments and your moral firmness."

"By no means offended, Colonel, or, I beg your pardon, 'General' I should have said. I only want to have the credit of being actuated by pure motives and apparently good reasons."

"I understand you, and now I suppose that I must forego the pleasure of having you on my staff?"

"My purpose is unchangeable, sir; though I seriously regret that you should be deprived of any pleasure on my account. I will strive, however, to elevate those of my rank, and hope to be the means of affording you some pleasure in this."

Every sentence Virtus added but tended to impress the General more and more with his high intellectual and moral worth; and hence his regret at the loss of such a friend from his immediate counsels.

"Well, then," said the General, "if you will not leave the ranks, you need not think that I have the less regard for you on this account. Nay, to tell you the truth, it even heightens my admiration for you. Now, you must allow me at least the pleasure of spending many social hours with you, for my own benefit. And when I need your counsel in any important military movement, I hope you will give it to me without reserve."

"Thank you, General; I will certainly cherish the thought with pleasure, that *you* are my friend; and should you ever need my advice in any matter, it will be cheerfully granted."

He then retired to his tent, leaving the General in silence to admire the character of one whose "price is above rubies."

The next day being Saturday, the regiments were all required to wash their clothing, and be in readiness for the Sabbath. It was about 10 o'clock, A. M., when under a shady bower of nature's own providing, one of Zion's sweet songs was sung by many a pious soldier. To a traveller ignorant of the fact that civil war had called many a brave man from the comforts of home, the present scene would have been taken for a regular camp meeting. The order was perfect, each regiment seated by itself, the whole forming a hollow square. At the root of a tree near the centre of the square was seated a minister of God whose face was radiant with Divine expression; and by his side the General, with several of his staff, was seated on the ground.

At length the minister arose and read the following hymn :

"Am I a soldier of the cross ?
A follower of the Lamb ?" &c.

in a manner well calculated to induce one to volunteer in the Divine cause. There was an unction and a pathos about his manner that I never witnessed before nor since.

Then the whole congregation joined in singing. The effect of the song was at once exhilerating and melting to the hearts of men who, but a few weeks before, were permitted to worship God with their dear friends at home.

The song over, a touching prayer ascended to the throne on high. Many a soldier joined in this prayer, and at its close quietly breathed a hearty " *Amen.*"

The preacher arose, opened his pocket Bible and read the text:

" *I have fought the good fight.*"

I shall attempt to give nothing more than a brief sketch of his sermon, for the simple reason that it would be impossible for me to do more. He said :

" My friends, we are engaged in a two-fold warfare ; one against the enemies of human liberty ; the other against the enemy of our souls. The former involves our interests for *time*—the latter, for *eternity*.

" We all know full well the causes which led to this temporal struggle. Our enemies disregarding all constitutional obligations, trampling under their feet our dearest rights, and in violation of all the principles of justice, reason and enlightened conscience, have forced us to leave our homes, with all their endearments, and meet them on these bleak mountain tops to interpose our lives between them and our nation's liberties. And considering the importance of the principles involved in the present struggle, who does not feel that no sacrifice of treasure or of blood is too great for him to make? There is not, I am persuaded, a man present, to whom the comforts and blessings of home would not be irksome, while the enemy threatens our borders.

" But, however great the interests involved in the present issue, they are extremely contemptible when compared with those involved in this warfare of which the inspired Apostle speaks in the text.

" The thing to be contended for in this great struggle, is *the soul—its eternal happiness or misery.* Every man that has a *soul* should be engaged in this warfare. Why should a man be so willing to secure redress from his temporal enemies—why should he be so prompt to resent a comparatively slight injury—when a numerous host, viler even than the Abolitionists have invaded the territory of the *soul*, and yet he does not impose the slightest resistance to their soul-destroying aggressions? Why so prompt to secure a temporary good, and yet remain careless of your eternal interests?

" I have said that in this great contest the *eternal interests* of *the soul* are at stake. This involves your *all.* If the battle goes against you, *infinite torture*, the loss of every desirable liberty. and indescribable woe, together with eternal slavery will be your lot. If successful. the indescribable bliss of heaven will be yours to enjoy for ever and ever. In this conflict there is *infinite evil* to be avoided, and *infinite good* to be secured.

" Let us now consider the forces engaged in this fearful struggle.

" Those who fight against the soul, are the Devil, (the commander-in-chief,) all the wicked spirits who are subject

3

to his control, the *world*, and the *flesh*. These, together, form a most formidable host !

" The Devil goeth about as a roaring lion, seeking whom he may devour ; or, if it suits his purpose better, he transforms himself into an angel of light. All the demon hordes are engaged in his service and ready to do his bidding. These evil spirits labor to ruin your souls.

" They use the world—its pomp, wealth, and promised pleasures, as a means to ensnare you. Many bright, though fatally delusive pictures, are held up before the mind, for the purpose of engrossing the affections, suborning reason, and bribing conscience.

" Then, again, the flesh—your own wicked desires, feelings, principles, passions and lusts—these are, perhaps, your greatest enemies.

" Now, imagine the devil using the world with all its fascinations, to inflame these passions, and what a host there is contending for your destruction !

" On the other side, Christ appears as your prime leader. The Holy Spirit is his 'Chief of Staff.' Angels are his faithful allies. All the faithful followers of the Lamb, whenever we 'take sweet counsel with them,' will embolden us for the conflict. Then, too, Reason and Conscience, Hope and Fear, are ready to lend their aid.

" The word of God, 'the sword of the Spirit,' informs us *when* and *where* we may expect the enemy, how we should make the attack, and points out the weapons we must use. This word also furnishes the key of the great Armory, where we can get the 'whole armor of God,' viz: The helmet of *salvation*, the shield of *faith*, the breastplate of *righteousness*, the girdle of *truth*, and the preparation of the Gospel as a protection for our feet. Thus armed, if we will advance with full confidence in our leader, and with humble prayer that he will protect us, the victory will be ours—victory here, and victory hereafter. And when the conflict is ended, we will be transplanted in the Paradise of God, where, through eternal ages, we will bloom in unspeakable glory!

"I as a commissioned officer, call for volunteers in this glorious campaign. Who will respond? Conscripts can never be admitted—you must *volunteer!* I promise you a large bounty of 'a conscience void of offence'—peace, happiness. Come and enlist under this noblest of all leaders, who is at once omnipotent, omniscient, and infinitely merciful, just and good."

Such were the prominent features of this remarkable sermon; yet to appreciate it fully, it was necessary to *hear* it, and *see* the speaker.

After the minister closed, the General arose, and made a few well-timed remarks. He fully endorsed what the preacher had said, and encouraged the men to enlist under the banners of King Immanuel. He furthermore stated:

"1st. That he, while in command, would require the proper observance of the Sabbath.

"2d. That there should be no drills of any character on the Sabbath.

"3d. That all would be expected to attend Divine service on Sabbath.

"4th. That gambling, drunkenness, profanity, stealing, &c., &c., would not be tolerated."

The large congregation, at the instance of the General, then arose and sang the following beautiful lines:

"On the mountain's top appearing,
Lo the sacred herald stands;
Welcome news to Zion bearing—
Zion long in hostile lands.
Mourning captive,
God himself shall loose thy bands," &c.

The assembly had but just dispersed, when a courier was seen advancing at full speed, from the direction of the enemy. He was probably not less than a mile in the distance when he was first seen. "What can this signify?"

CHAPTER II.

The courier found his way up the winding road to the narrow pass in the Gap, inquired for the General's head-quarters, and hastened to deliver his message. The news was highly exciting. The Colonels were at once summoned to the General's tent, and they "went into secret session." Having no "Aid," the General sent for Virtus. "If I can only get the aid of this young *nobleman*," said the General to himself, "I will not fear the face of the enemy."

The Colonels retired and Virtus entered.

"Come, now, friend Virtus, will you not act as my Aid—my Adjutant, rather, for a few days? I *need* your services."

"I greatly regret the sacrifice of a great principle; and next to this, I would regret to disoblige you honored sir."

"It is only for the present emergency that I require your services."

"But *principles* do not change with time," answered the other.

"True, yet 'time and occasions' may change one's duty."

"You can *detail* me as your Adjutant, if you like; but as to leaving my position voluntarily, that I will not do so long as I am in the service."

"Would you serve as faithfully under a detail as you would voluntarily?"

"I would *try* to do my *duty*, though I might not be able to do as well as if I should act of my own accord."

"I will risk that, if you will not become offended at the detail."

"I shall not be offended, sir, if you detail me ▬▬▬▬"

you think you can do no better, and if the detail is to last but for a *few days-*"

"You are detailed, then."

"The enemy," continued the General, are crossing over the mountain below us, and from all accounts will soon be in our rear, and cut off all communication with the Government. It is difficult to know what is best to be done. If we remain here, the probabilities are that we will be forced, for want of provisions. to surrender; if we evacuate the Gap, we surrender the key to this whole country. What think you?"

"I do not know what the strength of the enemy is. My action would be governed very much by this; if the enemy are not more than two or three to one, I should not evacuate this strong position."

"The enemy are reported 10,000 strong."

"Their *real* number, then, will not exceed 6,000; for numbers are usually much exaggerated. Our own strength, I should judge, is not far from 3,000. I should not retreat."

"What would you do?"

"I would dispatch one or more couriers to the railroad, and call for 5,000 men at once."

"But where can so many men be had?"

"There is just about that number at ——, and they can get here in 48 hours, by a forced march."

"Much better qualified to be a General than I am," thought the officer, as these words of wisdom fell from the private's lips.

"Would you order these reinforcements to come all the way to the Gap."

"No, sir; they should stop about 20 miles from this place, so as to close in upon the enemy if he turns upon us; or fall upon him if he makes his way to the railroad."

"But suppose these reinforcements should not be able to come?"

"That is hardly probable as they were at —— three days ago: and besides, I do not know where they could be needed more than in this military department."

The General had resolved on pursuing very much the course prescribed by Virtus, and now that his dearest friend in the army had, by his own keen intellect, pointed out the same course as that best to be adopted, he felt much confirmed in his plans.

"But," continued the General, "I must at once send some on to the railroad, to forward a dispatch for the troops; and this I regard as a most important service. Our very existence depends on the success of the courier!"

"Very important," said the other, "and I would send not less than three."

"I will send *you* the nearest rout, and two others by a different rout." Pointing to his fleet black steed, "he will carry you through safe—he can make the trip in six hours."

"Hand me your orders, and I will be gone—there is no time to be lost."

"The General snatched up a piece of paper and wrote as follows: "Brig. Gen. —— ——, Dear Sir:—The enemy are crossing the mountain South of us, for the purpose, doubtless, of cutting us off, or causing us to evacuate the Gap. Bring your troops to ——, on the first train, and then march out to ——, ✕ roads, 15 miles south of this place. Stationed at this point, you will be ready to meet the enemy, should he make for the railroad; or you will fall upon his rear, if he moves against us at the Gap. One of my Aids will meet you at said ✕ roads. Every thing depends upon your prompt movement.

Yours with anxiety,

—— ——. Brig. Gen. Commanding.

Concealing this note carefully about his person, Virtus, with two navy ropeaters "in pocket," mounted the black charger, and put off for the rail read. Other courier's were sent by different routes.

No one who has not himself been a courier in a tory country, can appreciate fully the dangers to which they are exposed. For the sake of saving a command, they often imperil their own lives.

Virtus was now to make a journey of 40 miles through the midst of tories and bushwhackers, and possibly, too, he might come in contact with the enemy. But his heart was brave enough to carry him wherever duty called him. No coward fear made him loiter on the way; and though his style of travel pointed him out as the bearer of important messages, and as a mark for every idle bushwhacker to shoot at, his noble heart, nerved with the justice of his cause, and supported by the arm of omnipotence, fluttered not at the idea of his dangerous adventure.

The noble steed descends the mountain slope in a sweeping gallop, proud of the manly rider that filled the saddle. On, on they went, unmolested, until they reached a narrow pass through a mountain spur, where precipitous rocks overhang the road. He had not gone far in the dark pass, before zip! zip! whistled the bullets near him. The report of the guns showed that the cowardly *whackers* were on the cliff of rock above him to the left. A savage yell from the barbarians had but pierced his ear, when two stalwart looking men appeared in the road before him, resolved, it seemed, to contest his passage with their lives! "What shall I do?" queried our hero as he popped the spurs deeper still into the sides of the dashing charger. "My *duty* requires me to *go*, and *go* I will, or my life shall pay the forfeit," was his stern resolve. Pulling out one of his repeaters and dashing forward at full speed, he determined to do them all the damage possible, even if he fell in the conflict.

When he approached within thirty paces of the enemy they raised their guns to fire; and at this instant the fearless rider "pulled down" on one of the wretches, and he fell. The other frightened at the sad fate of his comrade,

dropped his gun and darted for the bushes "for dear life."
Unfortunately for him, he was a little too late; for a ball
from the faithful repeater, struck him in the leg, and he
fell, crying at the top of his voice, " help! help!!"

With no one to dispute his passage, the hero on his foam-
ing steed, measured space at the rate of about a mile in
3 minutes. Nor was his heart devoid of gratitude to Him
who alone can save in the hour of danger. On he went
until he ascended a hill that furnished a view of the road
that lay before him. His keen eye soon scanned the road
as far as he could see it, and seeing no one to dispute his
passage, he drew in his reins, and resumed a more moderate
pace. Another hour brought him within view of a cavalry band of about, as best he could judge, one hundred
men, coming towards him. " Who are these?" questioned
the hero. "Their uniforms are those of the enemy!"
Quick as thought he wheeled around, and went back a few
paces. Looking back he saw the enemy coming after him
at full tilt, their sabers, meantime, making a noise that
would have paralyzed the valor of one less brave. Rein-
ing his horse out of the road he began to ascend the mountain side. Had he been riding a horse less nimble and
fleet than Selim, of revolutionary fame, he never would
have reached the top; but as fortune, or rather, Providence would have it, the snorting steed carried him safely
up the mountain height, which the enemy essaying to do,
found impracticable. They fired after him, but without
effect.

The mountain range ran very nearly parallel with the
road, though at too great a distance from it to endanger
him from the bullets of the enemy. Having gained the
top, he went on his way more leisurely. From an opening
in the green woods, he could occasionally see the road,
though it was impossible for him to reach it, if he had
even desired it.

For several miles he travelled over rough ledges of rock

that to one on a less important errand, and less determined to " make the trip," would have appeared almost impossible.

The sun was just about hiding itself behind the western mountains, when the hero discovered that he was nearing the road only a few yards from the spot where he was previously captured by the bushwhackers. Ten miles more, and he would be at the railroad. "I fancy now," said he to himself, "that I am out of the reach of bushwhackers. I will have an easy time the rest of the way."

But this belief did not throw him off his guard. His dark eyes took in not less than 100 degrees in his front; so thoroughly did he scan every lurking place suited for the enemy.

It was growing dusk when he hove in sight of the desired town. He soon reached the telegraph office, sent his important message, and received as an answer: "'O. K.' We will be up within four hours."

—————— ———— ———— Brig. Gen. Com'd'g.

It is difficult for one to imagine the pleasure which Virtus felt on receiving this reply. He felt that he had very probably been the means of saving his whole brigade from capture; and while he viewed the feat which he had performed, with complacency, he thanked God for that kind Providence which had saved his life, brought him through such dangers unharmed, and enabled him to perform a a work so beneficial to his command and to his country.

Riding up to a livery stable, he ordered his horse fed well, and rubbed for an hour. He then made his way to a hotel, where he got supper. While at the supper table, a stern looking old gentleman, who sat on the opposite side of the table, questioned our hero as follows:

" Do you belong to the army, sir?"

" I do, sir," was the reply.

" To whose command?"

" To Gen. ——'s."

" Where is he stationed?"

" At —— Gap."

" How many troops are there ?"

" I cannot tell you, sir."

" Are you ignorant of the number, or do you not wish to tell ?"

" I do not know precisely how many troops are there; and if I did, I would not be at liberty to tell."

" When did you leave the Gap ?"

" Not a great while ago, sir "

" You are not very communicative, sir."

" No sir."

" You certainly might afford to tell when you left the Gap."

" Sir, I must inform you, once for all, that I am much less communicative than you are inquisitive. I have no desire to offend you or any one else; but I don't like for a *stranger* to ask me so many questions."

" You are quite sensitive, young man; and doubtless feel your own importance as most soldiers do."

" You, sir, would be more important in my estimation, if *you* were a soldier, ready to meet the invaders of our country. As to my own opinion of myself, I have this to say : I am a little too prudent to tell my business to strangers, even if by refusing to do so, I gain their displeasure. I think too much of myself to be made a goose of," and with this, he gave the old man a glance that satisfied his curiosity, or at least served to check his impertinence.

The truth is, this same old man was a 'staunch admirer of Abe Lincoln; and carried the mail, secretly, from the tory families, and brought letters from the Northern army to them. He was apprised of the fact that the Yankee army was approaching, and he wished, if possible to find out whether the army at the Gap knew anything of their advance. Finding himself unable to succeed in gaining any information from our hero by the means already adopted, he changed his policy and began a different process.

" I did not wish, my dear sir, to offend you; nor to pry into your business. I am glad to find a soldier that can keep a secret. I think the more of you for this. Are you going back to the Gap soon, sir? I live between this place and the Gap, and would be glad to have your company."

" I have not determined precisely *when* I will return, nor in what direction. I have some matters of business to attend to, and may not be able to get back for several days. You say you live on the road between this and the Gap?"

" Yes."

" Immediately on the road?"

" No; about half a mile from the road."

Supper now over, the conversation ceased; yet the old man showed evident signs of uneasiness. He sought to protract the conversation; but he had no reason to hope that he could extract any valuable information from our well-guarded hero. This miserable tory knew that the yankees had passed over the mountain, and he feared that news had been brought of that fact. He resorted to one other trick, to ascertain, if possible, the object of the soldier's visit to town; and he accordingly inquired as follows:

" Do you know any thing of the whereabouts of the enemy that has threatened the Gap"

" I perceive, sir," answered the other, "that you are remarkably inquisitive. Allow me to ask you a few questions. Are you a Southern man?"

" I am; I was born and raised in the South.?"

" I don't mean that, sir; I mean, are you for the South in the present war?"

The old tory betrayed great confusion; but at length replied. " I am, sir."

There were several gentlemen sitting near, who heard his answer, and turned towards him in utter astonishment; for they all knew him to be opposed to the South, or, in other words, a tory. The old fellow, wishing to answer no more

questions, began to cough, and move towards the door. As
soon as he reached the door he stepped out, and began to
walk, and then to run, away as fast as possible.

Virtus, who had already suspected his loyalty, walked to
the door, and called to him to come back; but finding that
he would not stop, and suspecting that he was a spy, he put
off after him, and, being nimble of foot, soon overtook
him.

" Why are you running, sir ?"

" I find that I have overstayed my time already, and I
must hasten home."

" Not quite so fast, sir; you are my prisoner. Stop this
instant, or if you are not a dead man in a minute, you will
wish you had."

" Your prisoner !! What have I done, that I am to be
thus summarily arrested ?"

" We will inquire into that afterwards—come back with
me."

The tory turned to come back; for he knew that if he
did not obey the order, he would receive a ball in him right
soon. When they re-entered the house, the young man
delivered the prisoner over to some soldiers, to be well
guarded until an officer should take his case in hand.

Seeing the old man striving to shift some papers from his
pocket, he seized them, and, on examination, found that
he had several letters to tories in the yankee army. He
also found one letter giving very important information rel-
ative to the immediate movements of the enemy. He carefully pocketed the letter, and, privately, told the soldiers to
guard him as a *spy*, until a superior officer should call for
him. This they pledged themselves to do at all hazards.

He then called for a private room, to which he immediately retired. Having procured pen, ink, and paper, he
then addressed the following note to the General to whom
he had previously sent the dispatch:

Brig. Gen. ———— :

Sir,

Having been detailed on Brig. Gen. ————'s staff, I was at once dispatched to this place, to telegraph you the information which you received this evening. On my way to this place I encountered the enemy's cavalry. I think it certain that the enemy will move in force against the Gap to-morrow or next day. This I judge from the fact that I met their cavalry 12 miles this side of the Gap, proceeding in that direction. You will have to make all possible speed, to prevent the force at the Gap from being cut off.

I arrested a suspicious character in this place this evening, and found treasonable letters on his person. The guard will deliver him over to you.

I will leave within a few minutes for the Gap, and will do my utmost to have a messenger meet you at ——— X roads to-morrow by 12 m.

Your ob'dt serv't,

R. VIRTUS,
A. A. G. (pro tem.)

He closed his letter and went to get his horse. What an undertaking to attempt to go back to the Gap that night! The enemy's cavalry were certainly on the only road that he knew that led to his command. Bushwhackers were in great abundance; and very probably the enemy's infantry were encamped on the same road! But all this did not alarm our noble hero. He felt that he could face death itself, if duty required him to do so. Moreover, he knew that his life was in the hands of God, and that He could and would protect him, if He saw best to do so. And even if he should die, he had a bright hope of a glorious immortality beyond the grave, and that death would but hasten his perfect bliss. Why should one, " whose heart is stayed on God," fear danger? Why should one, whose happiness will but begin to dawn at death, tremble to meet the dread monster?

The heart of one less brave and religious, might well have quailed before the danger that lay in the path of the hero.

The noble steed, faithfully fed and rubbed, came out of his stall with head up, fully ready for the trip. One would hardly suppose from his looks, that he had carried his rider already forty miles that day, at the rate of eight miles per hour!

In the saddle, he lopes off " as supple as a fawn." Every eight minutes carry him a mile. He passed some persons, and met some; yet he halted not, until he arrived at the top of a high hill, near the place where the bushwhackers had captured him. Looking in the direction of the Gap, he saw the lights of the enemy's camp-fires, reflected on the mountain-side.

" What shall I do now ?" queried the hero, as he thought of the rough mountain-top over which he had escaped from the enemy a few hours before. To attempt to travel the road, would insure his capture.

It was a star-light night, and the moon would be up by 11 o'clock. " Possibly," thought he, " I may be able to make the trip. There is nothing like trying." Upon this he reigned his steed to the right, and began to ascend the mountain. The reader can hardly appreciate the difficulties in our hero's way, unless he is acquainted, from personal experience, with the rugged mountain-tops of the Cumberland or Alleghany range.

Slowly he felt his way along, sometimes walking and sometimes riding, until, after on hour's travel, he came within full view of the enemy's camps. He halted, and surveyed the fires with great particularity, designing to ascertain as nearly as possible the number of troops. He could distinguish the encampments of regiments. " There ~~are,~~" thought he, " ~~about~~ troops here. If things~~

well, they will either fall into our hands, or return over the mountain more rapidly than they came."

He resumed his dangerous course on the mountain-heights, and soon he discovered that the enemy's encampment extended as far as to the place where the road crossed the mountain-range on which he was traveling. He halted, calmly surveyed the prospect, and found that he must descend the mountain on the right, and, if possible, ascend the next range. Accordingly, he dismounted, and led his horse down the precipice. At times he found it almost impossible to prevent tumbling headlong down the mountain; but winding along, he at length reached a deep ravine between the two mountains. Cautiously he felt his way along, until at length he found an old road running along between the mountains. It would not do to follow this far, lest he should, on gaining the main road, come in contact with the enemy. He must begin, as soon as possible, to climb the mountain on the right. How this could be done, did not at first appear; for it seemed to be very steep. Slowly he moved along the road, in search of a by-path that would lead him up the declivity. He had not gone far when a dark form presented itself in the road before him! "Is this one of the enemy's pickets?" queried he to himself. "I am too close now to retreat," thought he; "so I will go on, and see what it is."

Having gone a few paces farther, he saw that it was a man, a soldier! "This cannot be one of our soldiers," thought he, "so I will prepare to defend myself." So pulling out his faithful repeater, he presented it on the man in front of him, and kept advancing. "Halt! halt!! halt!!! who come dar?" came from the excited Dutch picket, and he raised his gun to shoot. But before he had time to take aim, a ball struck him, and dropping his gun, he measured space very rapidly up the road toward the camp fires. Other forms arose before him, but panic-stricken, they all fled in wild confusion in the same direc-

tion. The yell raised by these retreating valiants, alarmed
the regiment that encamped some half mile distant, and
great confusion prevailed in their midst. It was not certain in the mind of our hero, whether the enemy were pre-
paring to retreat or advance; but finding a place where it
seemed possible to ascend the mountain, he began the ardu-
ous work. Slowly he labored his way up, until finally he
reached the top, where he could plainly see the enemy's
fires. About this time the moon began to peep over
the eastern hills, and cast her pale mantle of light over the
tree tops. The scene would have been admired in times of
peace; but the gloomy shadows of war have fallen upon
most of nature's beauties and eclipsed their glory!

It now became important for the hero to consult his
course, and decide in what direction to move. From his
elevated position, he saw that the mountain made a considerable curve, leaving the enemy far to the left. To
take one direction or the other, was his only alternative; so
he began to move on as fast as possible in the direction of
the curve, feeling assured that this would not lead him far
out of his way. Though the path was rough, he found
less difficulty in making his way, owing to the friendly influence of Luna. Grateful to him who holds in his own
hands the destiny of nations and of men, he hurried on
his way making about four miles an hour. He passed
within sight of the enemy's pickets, or cavalry, near the
place he had met them before, though not from the same
range of mountains, along which he had escaped early in
the evening. Going several miles farther, he began to descend, and after much difficulty reached the bottom, and
finally after going over another mountain, he reached the
road! "Thanks to Him who has been so kind as to guard
me safe thus far," soared to heaven on the wings of pure
gratitude. Who but God could have brought him through
so many dangers and so great?

At a sweeping pace he completed the rest of his journey,

reaching the General's head-quarters about half-past two o'clock, a. m., neither bushwhacker nor yankee annoying him. He found the General up and wide awake, no sleep having visited his eyelids during the night.

Virtus was met at the tent door, and greeted with as much cordiality as if he had been the "Commander in Chief." His noble head and generous heart were fully appreciated by the General, and his admiration for him was augmented by the fact that his friend's virtue and integrity were proof against all temptation. The price of such characters is far above rubies.

On entering the tent, Virtus handed the General the dispatches which he had received from General ——, which were read with much eagerness. The position and probable number of the enemy were then given; and the necessity of sending some one to meet the re-inforcements at daylight the next morning, was also laid before him. "It is all-important," said he, "that Gen. —— should have some instructions early to-morrow; for he will be within six or seven miles of the enemy by day-break."

"Is the enemy moving in this direction?" inquired the the General.

"There is no doubt of it," responded the other; "for their advance is with n twelve miles of this place, and their rear is this side the ✕ roads."

"I have been studying who shall be sent. It will not do to entrust this business to a common man; and to call on you to do it, would be asking too much."

"Have the other couriers returned?"

"I have seen nothing of them. Did you meet them at the railroad?"

"No, sir; they had not arrived there when I left."

"I fear they have been captured."

"It is quite probable."

"What would you advise me to do?"

"I have given you all the information at my command,

4

and I suppose you are able, of course, to decide what is best to be done."

"True; I have my plans; but these may be modified by suggestions from you. I hope never to reach a point in my military career, at which I cannot even change my plans when better ones are offered."

"But the world would think it quite strange, and even presumptuous, in me to be submitting plans to a *General!*"

"I care very little what the *world* thinks, unless it thinks right; but this it cannot do, when it excludes reason as properly exercising an influence over our plans. The fact that you persist in calling yourself a *private*, does not make your reason or judgment any less valuable to me. If you were a Major-general, your views would be none the more important. Military position neither adds to the value of a man's *reasons*, nor makes him a *man*. He must have *worth*, not of an *accidental*, but of an *individual* character, if he is worth any thing."

"This is all very true; and, allow me to say, I feel proud to serve under a general who takes this, the only sensible view of the subject. But, pardon me, sir; there is no time for discussion *now*. A courier should be sent at once to meet Gen. —— by day-break to-morrow morning. But as you have asked my views, I will give them in few words."

"If you please," interrupted the General.

"Well, then, a courier should be dispatched at once, to meet Gen. ——, with orders from you to press on the enemy's rear as closely as possible. By this means, there will be no chance for him to escape; for he is *now* this side of the road that takes him back the way he came over the mountain; yet the re-inforcements, after they gain the cross roads, should come on as rapidly as possible; not, however, to press them, or discover their pursuit until the enemy come near enough to attack your brigade.

"Then. again, I would send out one or more regiments about two miles from this place, where there is a remarkably strong position. With a few pieces of artillery, and a regiment to support it, the enemy can never advance to this place. Besides, that is a much better position for defence than this. When the firing commences at this point, as it probably will by 10 o'clock. a. m., Gen. ————'s forces can close upon the enemy's rear, and thus we will probably capture the whole force. This would be my programme."

" But what if the enemy should be advancing on the other side of the Gap?"

" Let them advance; one or two regiments, together with our heavy guns, will be ample to repel them."

" I am delighted," said the General, " with your programme; I have already planted a battery at the place you have mentioned, and a regiment is now in the vicinity of the place. The enemy has appeared on the other side of the Gap, but a few men will be ample to repel them. Your plan is about identical with mine. The courier is what troubles me! How is he to pass by the enemy?"

" Just as I did to-night. He can pass them before light."

" By what route?"

" He can travel the regular road twelve miles, then take the mountain on the left, and thus pass them."

" Will you suggest the name of some one competent to the task?"

" I can go myself, or try it, if you wish. The road is full of danger, and there is no time to be lost. Should the enemy start this way before day, as he probably will, there is a great probability of my being captured."

" But you are too much exhausted! My dear sir, you should not attempt it."

" I am rather fatigued ; but there is a great deal at stake, and now is the time for me to render my services, if they are worth any thing. I am willing to make the effort, if you desire it."

" I am convinced that no one could accomplish the difficult task so well: and if you will not think me willing to ride a free horse too hard, you may lay me under many obligations by going."

" Let me have your orders and a fresh horse; for it is high time I was going."

" You write the orders, and I will sign them."

Virtus then wrote a brief note to Brig. Gen. ————, containing the points previously mentioned, and the Gen. gave his signature. A fresh charger was brought up, a few refreshments put in his saddle-bags, and off he went in a sweeping gallop.

For a few miles he followed the road leading directly from the Gap; then, seeing that the enemy had already thrown out scouting parties, took to the mountain-paths.

He cautiously wended his way along the craggy peaks, overlooking the road to the Gap, now beginning to be filled with soldiers clad in " blue and gold."

He could see them indistinctly through the dim light of night, and when torch-light cast around a fitful glare. Taking note of every thing, he rode as swiftly forward as possible. Just before daylight, he came opposite the cross roads, where he discovered that the enemy had left some forces. They were soon passed; and as there was now nothing to fear, he quickly descended to the road, and pushed forward as rapidly as possible. Soon after daylight, he met the re-inforcements, and proceeded at once to deliver his dispatches to Gen;————.

While Gen. ———— was reading them, Virtus stood respectfully by; and when he had finished, said:

" The larger body of the enemy are on their way to the Gap now. A force not very large, I think, is at the cross roads."

"How did you pass them? I thought that the only way."

"So it is considered; but I found that a horseman could pass along the sides and top of the mountain, and came that way."

Hasty orders were issued, and the band moved rapidly forward. Gen. ———— determined to cut off, and, possibly, capture the guard at the cross roads. To effect this, he divided his command into three parts. Two of them, under competent officers, he sent forward—one on either side of the enemy. Thus he succeeded in completely surrounding them.

About half-past nine o'clock, the booming sound of cannon from the direction of the Gap was heard.

Very nearly at the same time, Gen. ———— closed round the force at the ⨯ roads, who prepared to make a vigorous resistance as the forces from behind came upon them; but when they found themselves hemmed in on all sides, they surrendered after a short struggle. Very few were killed or wounded on either side.

So soon as orders could be given, and a guard detached for the prisoners, Gen. ———— pushed on with his remaining force. The loud report of cannon, occasionally heard, served but to increase his eagerness to be going forward.

"Quick, men, let us be moving. Now is the time to fall upon their rear. Providence favoring, we will make clean work of the enemy this time."

Thus encouraging his men, they moved off with nimble step, forgetting that they had made a forced march, and had enjoyed no sleep the night before. A word of cheer from a superior officer, often tends to supply, temporarily, at least, sleep, rest, and rations.

Full five miles an hour were measured by this noble brigade, hurrying on to the rescue of their friends at the Gap.

The cannon had been booming for an hour or more, when volleys of musketry were distinctly heard in the direction of the Gap. This tended to heighten their enthusiasm, and accelerate their pace. No straggler fell out from this patriotic band; though many a yankee hireling was found here and there on the road-side, anxious to be paroled.

Virtus all this time had been riding along with the General and staff, saying very little except when interrogated. The General, finding that every thing was moving on as well as he could desire, and having been favorably impressed with his intelligent, dignified courier, summoned Virtus to him, when the following conversation ensued:

"Do you know any thing of the country over which the fight is now raging?"

"Yes, sir; I have passed the place several times."

"Describe it the best you can."

"The present battle-ground is two miles this side of the Gap. Our forces hold a position there that cannot be flanked. The mountain-sides on either hand are almost perpendicular. The gap through which the road runs, is not more than fifty yards wide. Our artillery rakes the road for nearly half a mile.

"The mountains on both sides of the road cannot be ascended, except here and there, for a distance of two and a half or three miles this side of our batteries."

"Good, exclaimed the General; and he sent his aids along the lines to cheer the men, while he continued the conversation with our hero.

"Are there any roads leading off from this, between us and the enemy?"

"But one, sir, and that leads to the right, though it is traveled very little; moreover, we will pass that road very soon—say within half an hour. There are, however, two or three ravines leading off from the road, through which small parties of the enemy might make their escape. There too the mountain-sides are not so steep generally as to forbid the idea of a footman's escape over them."

The General, astonished at the amount and accuracy of

the Courier's information, inquired of our hero if he was an officer.

"No, sir; only detailed as such. My place will be in the ranks, when this fight is over."

"You," said the General, "are competent to make a good officer; and as there is a vacancy in my staff, I should be pleased to have you as my Aid."

"Thank you, sir, for the implied compliment. My own General has offered me a position on his Staff, but, considering all things, I prefer the private's place."

"Wonderful! indeed!" exclaimed the General. "You are the first man I ever knew to decline office! Pray what are your reasons?"

"There are many other men more competent for office than myself, who *need* it more; then, again, a private has much less responsibility than an officer; moreover, I am unwilling that any should pay a higher price for liberty than myself; and, finally, the private's position is much better calculated to produce that meek and humble spirit, which, in my judgment, is of more value than all earthly honors."

"Well! well!" said the General, "I had never thought of that before. I will consider your reasons when I have more time."

It was now no time to discuss great moral questions. There was one continuous roar of musketry, the sound of which was occasionally swallowed up in the deeper, louder roar of cannon.

"Double-quick!" was the order. On, on they went, at a rapid pace, until the smoke from the battle field became visible; then "Halt," "halt," went along from regiment to regiment.

They had now reached a place where it was comparatively easy to ascend the mountain on either side of the road; so the General sent two regiments to the right and two to the left, designing to cut off the possibility of escape either way; while two regiments were left to press the enemy's rear.

Thus they advanced until they came upon the enemy's reserve, who, anticipating no danger from that direction, fled in wild confusion towards the front. To the frightened yankee hosts, the mountains seemed to be alive with men; and, for the first time, they began to see their danger. Coming within musket range, a deadly fire was poured into the invaders from the rear and on both flanks; while there seemed to be no chance for their escape.

The firing was very heavy beyond, on the direction of the Gap, so that it was evident that two battles were furiously raging. The enemy had appeared in considerable force beyond the Gap, and were trying to force our position, supposing that our principle force was engaged on this side. Line after line of the enemy was broken and repulsed. Deadly volleys of grape and canister were poured into their ranks; and the force on this side, being able neither to advance nor retreat, displayed the white flag. Meantime they were doing all in their power to escape through a deep ravine on the left of the road. This trick was soon discovered, and effectually frustrated by the two regiments that had been sent to prevent such a move. Probably not more than 1,000 of the whole force were so fortunate as to make their escape; the remainder, about 5,000, fell into our hands—400 killed, 2,100 wounded, and 3,500 prisoners. A large amount of arms and ammunition were captured. The enemy, on the other side of the Gap, unable to effect anything but the slaughter of their troops, gave way, and fled in confusion.

Our loss did not exceed 10 killed and 50 wounded. This was one of the most brilliant victories of the war.

Not content with leaving a Yankee South of the mountain, a few regiments were sent out to intercept those who had escaped. Nor was the expedition wholly fruitless, for towards night, several hundred of the heartless invaders were marched into camps.

The hearts of the pious, among the Confederates, were filled with gratitude to Him who giveth the victory to whom he will. Especially did the General and Virtus offer devout thanksgiving to God for His great goodness. When night came, Virtus was sent for, to visit his General's headquarters. (He had reported to the General before, but as there was another General present and a number of officials, he retired as soon as possible.) On entering the tent, Virtus saluted his General and the General with whom he had travelled a good part of the day.

"Allow me, Gen. —— to present you with my Adjutant, Capt. Virtus."

Virtus bowed gracefully, touching his cap. "I had the pleasure," said the other, "of traveling in company with this gentleman to-day; and I assure you that he is entitled to our praise and gratitude for the valuable services rendered,"

"Pardon me," said our hero in an earnest manner, "I am not a Captain—am only a private as I told you to-day. Nor am I *ashamed* of the name."

"We will adjust that matter hereafter," said his General; "come now, and tell us of your adventures."

Virtus, averse to "blowing his own horn," said: "I managed, through a kind Providence, to make my way by the enemy, reached the General here as soon as I could, delivered your orders, or messages, and came back with his forces. I am too sleepy and tired now, to enter into details. Please excuse me unless you have some specific orders."

Saying this, he began to retire, when the General said, "Tarry with us to-night—I will make room for you, if I have to give you my bed. I sent for you, not for my own or the interest of the crowd, but to make you as comfortable as possible. So you will, I hope, spend the night with us."

"Thank you General; but you have company which it becomes you to entertain; and, besides, I have comfortable lodging in my mess."

"I have no company, sir, whom it becomes me to entertain more than yourself, however kindly I will entertain the General and his staff; for to no one more than to yourself, is due this brilliant success which has crowned our arms."

"I have done nothing more than my duty, which I am always ready to do," was the dignified reply. "Now, if you will excuse me, I will go to my tent."

"Certainly, if it is your wish; though I would decidedly prefer that you would stay."

"Propriety as well as comfort suggests that I should go. Good evening, gentlemen." Saying which, he gracefully bowed himself out, and went to his tent where gentle sleep was waiting to bestow genial repose upon the wearied hero.

Virtus had but left the tent, when his General said to his guest, "This is the most remarkable young man I ever saw. All the virtues are beautifully blended in his character! I never had the pleasure of being acquainted with so noble a character, or one more intelligent and refined. Competent to be a General of the highest order, he persistently refuses all promotion; nor is it in my power to answer the arguments with which he justifies his refusal."

"I was much struck with the young man, as we rode on together to-day," said the other; "and there being a vacancy on my staff, I politely tendered him the position of Aid de Camp; but he as politely declined it, and, as you say, bolstered his position with arguments which, at the time, I was unable to answer. He is a religious youth, I opine?"

"Yes, sir; one of the most pious I ever knew. His religion is not a mere *abstraction*, which is too often the case with professors; but it is a living, active principle with him. All his words, principles, feelings and actions, are adjusted in accordance with the word of God. In a word, he has the best rounded and the best developed character I ever knew."

"Suppose you send for him to-morrow morning, and we will argue the case farther with him; for with me, as I perceive it is with you, there is no obstacle in the way because of his inferior position."

"No," said the other; "it is *worth* that makes the man— *personal worth*, not circumsta........ honors. I will, at your request, send for him, to-morrow morning; but before dismissing this subject, permit me to tell you the part he has acted in the present campaign."

He then went on to relate all that he knew about the matter, which was listened to with the deepest interest by his distinguished guest. Among other things allusion was made to the capture of the spy at the railroad, when the letter which our hero had taken from the person of the spy was produced and read. From this it was ascertained that the enemy would not have advanced against the Gap, but returned over the mountain, if the spy had returned to the Yankee General; for there was a clause in the letter which the traitor had in possession, which read thus: "If there is any prospect of reinforcements being sent to the Gap, report the fact to me immediately; but if there is no danger, as I presume there is none, you can report to me at your leisure."

After expressing their high appreciation of our heroe's labors, and admiration of his character, the conversation turned on other matters, and finally they retired for the night.

Much refreshed with sleep, they arose early the next morning. Breakfast ready, Gen. B—— sent for Virtus, who appeared in a moment, and after the usual salutations, &c;, was invited to take a seat at the table.

"Thank you, General," said he; " my own breakfast

will be ready soon, and my mess will expect me.   Excuse
me; I must return."

" It can make no difference with your mess if you eat
with us; besides, I will send them word where you are.
We wish you to be with us for the pleasure of your company."

" Thank you; I will grant the request, though in doing
so, I do not wish it to be understood that I think it an
honor to be called from my own messmates."

" We understand that perfectly," replied the General.

When all were seated at the table, the visiting General,
turning to Virtus, said, " I think I am able to convince
you that you are in error with regard to your objections to
becoming an officer."

" Very well, s r; if you can, I will readily yield my
position, and accept office when it is tendered; for who is
a *fool* but him who acts contrary to *reason ?*"

" I would hear your objections again," said the General,
" and we will consider them one at a time."

" My first objection is, That privates make the greatest
sacrifice for liberty, and are, therefore, entitled to the
greatest honor."

" But do they *receive* it ?" inquired the General.

" This question has nothing to do with my proposition.
One proposition at a time, if you please."

The General perceiving the force of the objection, made
the following inquiry: " Was any private in General
Washington's army, deserving of more honor than the
General himself."

" As to that I cannot tell, sir, since I was never fortunate enough to see either the ' Father of his country,' or
any of the veterans whom he had the honor to lead."

" *Who* is to decide the amount of honor due a private or
an officer ? and *who* is to award it ?   If the people are to
be the judges, then I am sure that officers will be deemed
worthy of most honor; and if you do not submit the mat-

ter to the judgment of the people, to whom will you submit it?"

"To justice, the goddess of liberty, and to those whose views are just."

"But 'justice and the goddess of liberty' are mere abstractions, and are capable of giving no decisions and awarding no honors; and the 'just' to whom you refer are too far in the minority to be heard."

"You do not maintain that there is no standard of *justice* which tests the merits of every profession or occupation of man? And are you prepared to say that there is no principle of patriotism, which ascribes the greatest honors to him who sacrifices most for his country? Surely you will not teach such doctrines. There would be such great principles in existence even though the *whole* human family were so corrupt as not to see them. And as to the fewness of those who do do perceive them, and whose opinions are so far just. I would merely say, *the just have ever since the fall of Adam, been in the 'minority.'* According to your principle, a man should always look to see where the majority stands, before he assumes his position; and this, carried to an extreme, would, I have no doubt, take him to perdition."

"Much of what you say is true; yet it remains to be shown that a man should always shape his course in accordance with mere abstractions."

"You will please state what part of what I have said, is *not* true."

The General hesitated.

"Now, while you are making up your mind on this subject, I will state, as a universal axiom, that it is always right to be governed by principles of right, whether many, few, or none (besides the actor) perceive those principles."

"You have your *notions* about this; but let us have another *reason.*"

"I have given you *one reason*, and you have not been

able to answer in; yet, as you request it, I will give you an other. It is this: *The position of a private tends to humiliation, while that of an officer tends to self-exaltation.* Here the argument is two-fold, and both in favor of the private's position."

"Does not an humble position tend to degrade a man, and an exalted one elevate?"

"The *private's* position, I said tends to humble a man; you will please confine yourself to the argument."

The General was evidently at a loss to answer his argument; and General B—— generously came up, at this juncture, to reinforce him; hoping to defeat Virtus by a "flank movement." So he introduced a new argument altogether.

"I know," said he, "that you believe in the direction of Providence. Now has not Providence clearly opened up before you the way to office? May you not be acting sinfully in declining office thus providentially offered you?"

"A masked battery!" exclaimed Virtus; "yet I don't think it will cause me to 'change my base.' But seriously. I don't think that Providence ever opens up the way before a man, until all the *solid objections* to traveling that road, have been removed. It might be in my power to appropriate millions of gold belonging to another; yet while the commandment, 'Thou shalt not steal,' looks me in the face, I will not be justified in stealing it. While Providence may, and I think does have some general superintendence over everything—good and evil—that happens, I do not understand that He approves them all. The Captain of a vessel dare not follow in the direction of every breeze."

Finding that there was no chance for them to dissuade him, the visiting general said, "Well, my dear sir, if you will not attach yourself to my staff, I will be delighted to see you at my head-quarters at any time."

"Thank you, sir; when it is compatable with my duty, it will afford me pleasure to call on you, and if you entertained the same notions of merit that I do, I would invite you to *my quarters;* but I would not offend you by making any such invitation."

" No offence, sir, I assure you."

" Then I invite you to come."

" With great pleasure, whenever I visit this brigade."

" How noble a youth !" thought the generals His moral principles, they both felt, were purer than " gold seven times refined."

The conversation seemed likely to end at this point, when Virtus, wishing to " drive a nail in a sure place," said, " I hope, gentlemen. you will pardon me for alluding to one other subject connected with official position in the army "

" Certainly," replied both the generals, " we will be glad to hear from you."

" Well, then," said he, " it is this : Officers speak much of the *honor* attached to office, but rarely refer to the *responsibilities* which it imposes, if indeed they ever think of them.

" As I do not wish to deal in abstractions, I will, with your permission, allude to *some of your responsibilities.* Then—

1. You are responsible, largely, for the efficiency of your men—their *health, dress, drill,* &c.

2. You are responsible, to a great extent, for their *moral* deportment, as well as their gentlemanly bearing.

3. Their religious interests, also, are committed, in a fearful sense, to your care.

In a word, their efficiency as soldiers, their intellectual, moral, and religious interests—their interests for *time* and *eternity* are given, in a great degree, into *your* hands.

To be able to meet these *responsibilities,* officers should be *men*—men of sterling moral worth, of great energy, of decision, and intellect, and, above all, of eminent piety. Looking to all these requisitions and grave responsibilities, every officer should, in the language of Inspiration, inquire, " *Who is sufficient for these things ?*"

" I beg you, gentlemen, to think of your *responsibilities* as well as your *honors.*"

The generals both listened with the profoundest respect to these solemn truths, and Gen. B—, especially, showed signs of trouble within—he *felt* the force of the admonition. The thought flashed across his mind, " Through my neglect of duty, some young man's *morals,* and possibly his *soul,* may be lost. In that event, all earthly honors that I might win, would be infinitely contemptible, and worse than nothing."

The other officer, while a man of moral character, was not a professor of religion ; and, though he admitted the truth of most that our hero had said, he objected to one point.—Said he, " I am no professor of religion, and I don't think that I am responsible for the religious welfare of my men, as if I were a Christian."

" Whose fault is it, General, that you are *not* a Christian ?"

" My own, I suppose," (for his own conscience would not let him give a different answer).

" If it is your fault, then, that you are not a Christian ; and if, as you virtually admit, you *ought* to be a Christian, it is very plain that you are to blame for not doing those things which a Christian *ought* to do."

" I see it," said he, " and will *try* to meet the issue, by becoming a Christian as soon as possible."

This he said, not so much from a feeling sense of his own need of salvation, as that he might be able to discharge his duty to others ; for he clearly saw that he could not meet his moral and religious obligations to his men without true and undefiled religion.

" I hope," said our Christian hero, " that you will be successful in your efforts. But do you, General, *feel* the need of personal salvation ?"

" I feel, sir, that I cannot discharge my *duty* without being a Christian."

" Your duty to whom ?"

" To the soldiers under my command."

" Your *first* duty is to *God*. You must fee' your need of personal salvation—forgiveness through the merits of Christ, or you cannot become a true Christian. You must be more concerned to propitiate the favor of Him Whose authority you have, up to this time, despised, than to do any thing else."

The General evidently did not *feel* that load of guilt which all must feel, before they are willing to be saved by Christ. "I will study the matter, and do the best I can," was his reply to what Virtus had said.

The conversation was here interrupted, and Virtus returned to his tent. Gen. B— felt more like resigning his position than ever before ; for a sense of his responsibility was now so much impressed upon him, that he could hardly consent to remain longer in his position. While musing over the subject, the following thoughts lodged in his mind : "I am, in an important sense, responsible for the *dress, cleanliness, health, military efficiency, manners, morals,* and even the eternal welfare of my men ! If, through *negligence, wilfull ignorance, bad example,* or *undue toleration,* my men should suffer in their *physical, mental, moral,* or *religious* interests; the loss will be irreparable! To be the means of ruining the morals, manners, and especially the *souls* of those who are largely subject to my control, would eclipse all my military glory, and would be a disaster of such magnitude as that, were all the honors of the world to be heaped upon my head, they would appear as naught and vanity.

" I will do the best I *can* while I remain an officer," was his firm resolve ; "and I pray that God may give me grace to perform my *whole* duty."

Would that every officer could feel just as he felt. Then

would we see less of *hollow, swell-headedness;* then would we see officers competent to lead their men, not only to victory, but into the paths of moral refinement; then the army, instead of being a bedlam, (as is often the case,) would be a place of refinement, and the uneducated masses would be elevated and immeasurably improved by their connection with the army; while the wealthy, brought to feel some of the hardships of life, would have more correct notions of what a man *ought* to be, and an abiding sympathy for the poor. Then when peace shall spread her balmy wings over our beloved Confederacy, our soldiers who survive the bloody struggle for independence, would return to their homes, not vagabonds, blackguards, and blasphemers, but *gentlemen*.

CHAPTER III.

The enemy being overcome, there was no necessity for Gen. —— and his brigade to remain longer at the Gap. Therefore, after resting and enjoying the pure mountain air a few days, they returned to their old station on the railroad, that they might be ready to re-inforce where they were most needed. Their late experience had made them happy and hopeful. One success buoyed them up so they would be desirous of others, and would fight for them.

" How much confidence those men at the Gap have in their officers," remarked one of the Colonels to Gen. ——, while on their way back to the railroad.

" Yes; and how perfectly do both men and officers conduct themselves. I was charmed with Gen. B—'s brigade, and could but hope that mine, in which I have prided myself, would one day equal it," replied the General.

" Every thing," said the Colonel, " went on as steadily and smoothly as clock-work. I do wonder how so many steady men happen to get together."

" Quite likely, they were no better, as a whole, at first, than many other brigades. They have been made what they are. Gen. B— is no ordinary man. He understands how to fill his position."

" I fully concur with you there. His very appearance bears testimony to that," replied the Colonel.

And they were right in this Gen. B — had, from his first accession to office, deported himself in such a way as to gain the love and confidence of the good and wise, and to

inspire with fear those who were not disposed to obey army
regulations. As a colonel, he had strictly enforced the
army regulations. Morality was enjoined on all, and religion, outwardly, at least, observed. Himself a devout
Christian, he set a good example to those who were connected with him, and ever gave assistance to whatever
would tend to increase piety in his regiment.

When called to fill a higher and more responsible office,
he lost none of his religious zeal, but rather strove to be
more pious, that his increased influence might only be good.

The Sabbath he set apart as a day of prayer and worship. No reviews or drills were permitted, that he could
possibly prevent. The Army Regulations sustained him
in this; and if they had not, he would have preferred following the laws of a living God to those of men dead in
trespasses and sins. He conversed often and freely with
the Chaplain about the best means of spreading religion
among the men, and assisted him in his good work.

Seeing his goodness, the men could but admire and love
him, and consequently were delighted to please him by their
obedient and gentlemanly deportment.

The good Chaplain would be mistreated were we not to
state that he faithfully attended to his duties. Like a min-
istering spirit, he went from tent to tent—even from man
to man—pressing upon all their religious duty.

In such a brigade, of course stealing, or "pressing" without proper authority, was not allowed. If necessity demanded the impressment of a man's goods, full compensa-
tion was made him. A mere pittance was desirable to
stolen dainties.

Citizens gladly awarded the good general and his men
the meed of honesty; nor were they slow to show their
appreciation of such defenders.

Both privates and the lower officers vied with each other
in paying that strict regard to the military rules, that rendered the duty of those higher in office comparatively easy.

They were proud of their brigade, and strove to act in such a way as that others might imitate them advantageously.

Our hero-private, Virtus, was not the only one who was brave, honest, upright; but he, perhaps, was better than the majority, in that his intellect and heart had been uniformly cultivated. Gen. B— acknowledged him his own equal, and, as has been seen, was glad to introduce him to his brother officers. His arguments for remaining a private could not be answered. Though averse to assuming the responsibility of an officer himself, he delighted to see good and worthy men promoted.

A few days after the departure of Gen. —— and his brigade, Gen. B— summoned Virtus to him. After the customary salutations, the general said:

"I sent for you, to ask if you knew any good man capable of filling the position I have so urged upon you. Having set my heart upon having you, I find it difficult to select another."

"I can but continue thanks for your kindness in my behalf, for such, I am sure, you intend;" began Virtus. But the general interrupted him, to say:

"I must confess, my friend, that I am somewhat selfish too. Your good I certainly desire, but the greater benefit would result to myself from your acceptance of this office."

"That is certainly flattering to my vanity; but you will not feel the loss of my services, if those of a competent man be secured. Such a man, I think, I can name;" was the reply of Virtus.

"Who is he? and where to be found? I am ready to confer the office on him from your recommendation."

"I would not have you do so merely on account of my recommendation. You ought to feel fully satisfied of his competency to fill office, first."

"Of that I am satisfied, if you judge him so. But who is he?" again, enquired the general.

"It is Inman, of Company C; Col. H—'s Regiment."

" Inman ; I cannot recollect him.   Why do you recommend him ?"

" Because he is worthy ;" was the reply.

" Particularize, if you please."

" Then, 1st. He is a man of cultivated intellect; 2d.
His military genius is good ; 3d. He is brave.   He can
face the enemy, and has also great moral courage; 4th.
He is a poor man.   His family is barley able to subsist on
what his wife can earn.   Office would enable him to do
something for them ; 5th. He is a pious man—a man of
prayer."

Virtus would have given other reasons, but the above
were considered quite sufficient by the General, who begged
that he would at once introduce his friend.   To this Virtus
replied :

" I can hardly consider him a friend yet; though I would
like to.   I have only conversed with him a few times."

" How then do you know him to be fit for the office for
which you recommend him?" inquired the general

" I have had frequent opportunities of observing him,
and have confidence in what our mutual friends testify in
regard to him."

" But why not take this opportunity of helping so me
one of your own friends to office ?   You surely have friends
who would gladly accept," said the general, for the sake, it
would seem, of detaining our hero.

" True ; perhaps many of them would be glad of promotion, but I know of none who would fill the position more
creditably than he of whom I spoke.   Besides, I am not
one to have my friendship sought, because I may be able
to benefit in such ways.   I hope my reasons for recommend-
ing Inman were good."

" Yes, and perfectly satisfactory ; and now you may bring
in my new Aid.   I am anxious to form his acquaintance."

To the surprise and gratification of all, the new Aid hap-

pened to be one whom Gen. B— had noticed and compli-
mented in the late battle. Thus the office was at last satis-
factorily disposed of.

The remainder of the short stay—for it proved short—
was very pleasantly spent.

The occasional capture of a bushwhacker was all of news
they had. Hence there was ample time to explore the
mountain caves, and notice the freaks of nature so bounti-
fully lavished around the spot.

But these quiet, pleasant occupations were rudely broken
in upon. Ever faithful to his military duties, General B—
soon discovered the determination of the enemy to make a
flank movement. A large body of yankees were making
their way through a more eastern gap, with the evident in-
tention of cutting off all supplies, and compelling the surrender of the Gap.

Gen. B— communicated with his superior officers, advis-
ing them of his dangerous position. The way to the railroad was now beset with many dangers, and more than once
Virtus was detailed on the yet unfilled staff, to perform this
hazardous trip.

Though several times followed by the mountain robbers,
he managed to elude them. One visit to their encampment
had been sufficient to satisfy him, it would seem, from the
quick alertness which never forsook him, while away from
his command.

After much consulting and putting together "wise
heads," it was decided advisable for the Gap to be evacu-
ated. This our noble brigade were much averse to doing.
Yet, even this, was preferable to falling into the hands of
the enemy.

Every thing that could be removed was hastily put under
way ; while the remainder was as nearly as possible destroyed. Some of the larger guns were necessarily left behind, but in such a condition that they would require considerable repairing before they would work.

Less joyfully, because they were retreating, than when
they went up to the Gap, did the men leave it. Their jests
and mirth were laid aside, for the time, and something
of sadness took their place. But once more aboard the
cars, something of the old spirit returned; and hoping to
be the victors yet, they began to notice the country through
which they were passing.

"This place looks very much like an old friend," said
one to Virtus, as they neared a village.

Virtus blushed, stammered forth a reply, and was turning away when the other exclaimed: "Oh, I remember
now. This is where that beautiful young lady gave us
such delicious cakes. Don't you remember, Virtus? I
am going to look out and see if she is here to-day;" saying which, he hastened away without noticing Virtus'
deepening blushes, or waiting for an answer to his query.

Our hero was glad to be relieved of his friend's company just then. Truth is, he had recognized the station, and
was looking about him for a convenient place of observation. Just as he had secured a seat which commanded a
view of the station, he was summoned to the General's car,
which was in the rear. Something akin to vexation
troubled him when he heard the summons, for he would
probably lose the privilege of looking out. Yet he had
too high a regard for his General to delay obedience, so
arose and went at once to him. As he had anticipated, he
had little opportunity of outward observation; but he got
one glance at the beautiful mansion, and thought he saw
a lady at one of the windows, but as the conversation was
directed to him at the time, he could not console himself
with another glance. After talking over some of his plans,
and hearing the suggestions of his Aids, and of Virtus,
Gen. B—— suddenly exclaimed:

"As I live, here is our stopping place. I did not know
time was passing so rapidly."

At this announcement the heart of Virtus certainly beat

more rapidly than it was wont to. "Perhaps," thought he, "I may see *her*—may know *her* yet. It cannot be more than ten miles to ——. I am very glad we are to stop here at any rate. Who knows what may happen."

Thus musing, he mingled with the busy throng who were hunting blankets, knapsacks, &c., preparatory to leaving the cars.

Their encampment was in a beautiful wood near the rail road. A small river flowed sluggishly along on one side, while on the other beautifully cultivated fields stretched away.

They had been here only a few days, when it was discovered that the enemy were making great efforts to reach the railroad at that point. Their object could, of course, only be conjectured. The burning of the bridge over the river might have been their sole object—since that would tend greatly to interrupt our movements. But some thought that the devastation of all the surrounding country would result, if once an entrance was effected.

Gen. ·B—— used every precaution in his power to make his position secure. Pickets were kept out constantly and urged to be very vigilant. Only a few days elapsed before Virtus was sent out on the road leading northward. He was sauntering leisurely along, about two miles from camp, when he saw approaching, a lady accompanied by two servants.

As she came nearer, he perceived that it was she who, though unknown, had awakened emotions which, if not those of love, he could not account for.

"Now," thought he, "if I only had some excuse for detaining her, how fortunate would be my lot. But unless she stops of her own accord, I do not see any way in which I could gallantly speak to her." Thus he mused as she rode up and much to his gratification drew in her reins near him. A rosy blush suffused her fair cheek when she looked upon Virtus; and he, seeing that she recognized

him had scarcely enough composure left to make her a
graceful bow.

"Will you direct me to Gen. B——'s head-quarters?"
was the request of the fair lady; and never, at least so
thought Virtus, did mortal possess so sweet a voice.

"With pleasure, and moreover, I would gladly conduct
you hither, were I permitted to leave my post;" he replied
in a most courteous voice.

"Thank you. I see you are a picket, and know what is
required of you. If my horse will only remain quiet, I
shall get along well enough with directions."

"He does look too gay for a lady. Allow me to fix this
rein," said he, unfastening two buckles while fastening one.
Then they had to be fastened, and he persisted in doing it,
though the polite servant stood by ready to perform the
task.

"I have not often had the courage to mount him, but
father was anxious for us all to leave home to-day, and the
carriage would not conveniently hold us all, so I ventured
to come on before," said she.

"Are you leaving on account of the expected invasion?"
respectfully inquired our hero.

"Yes. Father could not safely remain himself, and will
not permit any of the family to be left behind. We expect
to have everything destroyed, but our greatest regret is in
leaving the home and grave of dear, dead mamma." A
tear flashed in the beautiful eye at these sad remembrances.

Virtus expressed his sympathy, and seeing that he could
no longer dally over the bridle, courteously asked one other
question, viz - "How far do you intend going?"

How his heart beat in the moment that he awaited the
answer. If she should be going any great distance, who
could tell if they would ever meet again?

The blush deepened on her cheek as she replied: "Only
a few miles south, to an uncle's. But you have not given
me directions to the General's head-quaaters yet."

With a glow of the cheek as deep as her own, he directed her in a few words. Then while each crimsoned deeper, they exchanged bows and "good mornings," and she passed on her way. The picket leaned upon his gun very unlike a vigilant soldier, while the lady's form was distinguishable among the trees. Nor need he be censured, if for a time, he thought more of the scene through which he had just passed, than of his duty as a soldier. He considered it one point gained to have heard her speak; another to know that she would not be many miles distant. He hardly dared, yet could but hope that the way for a more permanent acquaintance might soon be openened; but how, he would not even conjecture.

When, soon after, the sound of an approaching carriage was heard, he was not startled, or surprised, for he was expecting it.

"Now," said he, "I will see the family of that charming young lady, and it may be, learn her name."

The carriage soon came up, and the picket was not in the least chagrined at seeing it stop. A glance showed the occupants through the open window. They were an old lady of perhaps eighty years, a saucy school girl, and two sprightly children—a boy and girl—of the ages of seven and five years, respectively.

"Her grandmother, sisters and brother," interpreted the beholder to himself. The old lady looked out, and after bidding him "good morning," said:

"Has a young lady passed here this morning?"

"Be a little more definite, if you please. Several ladies have passed, and were I to 'answer affirmatively, I might not satisfy you;" said Virtus "catching at a straw," to hear the name of the fair unknown. The youngest child here used her privilege of being "pet," and answered before her grandmother:

"It is Auntie ——. Don't you know her? She is good and sweet and—"

"Hush, Grace; don't you see Grandma is trying to speak?" interposed the boy.

"I should say the gentleman would be greatly enlightened by your chatter," closed in the school girl, good humoredly nudging the little ones.

"Don't Aunt Lina," called out both children, while Virtus was thinking, "I was wrong, these little ones are not her brother and sister; but 'Lina,' as they call her, must be a sister—the striking likeness shows that."

"There, there, children, hush," said the old lady, enjoining silence. "You see," continued she, to Virtus, "spoilt children. I cannot help petting and playing with them, so they are ever ready to place themselves on an equality with me. They are all motherless, and for the sake of my lost daughter, they are tenderly loved. But old woman like, I am telling you things that I have no business to. I hope you will not feel fretted."

"I am not in the least, let me assure you," was the reply.

"A good young man, I doubt not. The lady I asked about is a grand-daughter also, a sister of this one," said she, laying her hand on Lina. "She was on horseback. Her name is ——. Do you know whether or not she has passed?"

"She has—at least, I think so." "Was she accompanied by two servants?"

"Yes, a man and woman."

"The man is mine. I call him my fortune," put in little Jo, in an important manner.

"She has passed, madam," said Virtus to the old lady, and then, to the boy. "Yes, he looks like a fine servant."

At this point little Kate drew out from her basket some tempting little cakes and offering them, said:

"Aunt Lina is ashamed to offer you any cakes because you look so nice, and like you had plenty to eat; but I

ain't 'cause Auntie —— says, the soldiers don't get anything *very* good to eat. Wont you have these ?"

"Yes, to please you, I will take them. They will make,
with my bread and bacon, quite a dinner," smilingly replied he.

"There, I am proud. I know I have done right," joyfully exclaimed the little girl.

"Indeed, you have, Kate. And I wish we could give
the gentleman enough to last him a week; but we had to
leave so hurriedly that we brought none but a small lunch-
eon with us," said her grandmother.

"Then I will not deprive the little girl of these—" began he, but she interrupted him to say :

"O yes, you *must* keep them. I would not take them
for any thing."

"O yes, keep them and take some more, then we will
have enough. We are not going far. You must come
to see us right soon, and we will try to make you enjoy
yourself."

"Come next Thursday, it is my birthday, and I always
have lots of candy, then ;" said Kate.

Virtus thanked her, and they all laughed. After
inquiring his name and apologizing for the familiarity of
the children, by saying that they knew whom to like,
the old lady ordered the driver to proceed.

Virtus congratulated himself not a little on his signal
success.

The form of the fair maiden now found a permanent
lodgment in his mind; so that, if he had been disposed
to do anything not in accordance with strict morality
and propriety, the presence of so pure a model of the
gentle sex would have restrained him. But our hero
needed no such aid to virtue; his principles, moral and
religious, were so correct as to make it, with the assistance of his Heavenly Father, quite easy for him to tread
the path of duty. It is only such minds as this that

can fully appreciate perfect specimens of grace, elegance
and virtue; for where low, vulgar passions infest the
mind, they blunt the perception of the pure, or, in other
words, these degraded passions are to the mind what
smoke is to glass—they destroy its transparency, and,
to that extent, shut out the beauty of objects without.
While *swine* have no appreciation of the value of pearls,
" worth appreciates worth."

The hours fled swiftly while our hero feasted his mind
on the beauty and loveliness of the peerless damsel;
yet, as is always the case with those whose hearts have
been pierced by the arrows of Cupid, he was not wholly
free from anxiety. The suspense, not to say uncertainty,
which envelopes the *new* lover, especially, is often very
painful. Still, in the present case, the unhappiness naturally consequent on suspense, was very much modified
by the sacred influences of religion. " All things work
together for good to those that love the Lord," thought
our hero; "and He has said, ' A good wife is of the
Lord.' I will entrust this important matter to Him,
and abide His decision. I will make my will bend to
His. Thus, I feel assured, ' all will be for the best;'
if the fair stranger is one day to be my bride, I trust
it will be for the mutual good of both, and for the decla-
rative honor of God; but if it would be better for us
never to see each other again, ' so mote it be.' "

It is natural for one thus impressed with a sense of
the Divine goodness, and whose heart is imbued with a
sense of obligation to God, to bear suspense, persecution,
adversity and hardships, without a murmur.

His picket hours being numbered for the present,
Virtus, with his comrades, returns to camps. He had
not been there a great while when Gen. B—— sent for
him, to appear at his head-quarters. Obedient to the
summons he appeared in front of the General's tent.

" Good evening! Come in !" heartily exclaimed the

General. Virtus saluted the General, and, like a true soldier, entered the tent, and took a seat, the superior officer
handing him a camp stool. While the General had none
but gentlemen on his staff, not one of them held so high
a place in his confidence, respect, and affections, as Virtus.
When any nice point, whether of strategy or morals, came
up, Virtus must be consulted; and his staff officers present,
knowing the General's fondness for being alone with Virtus,
gracefully retired.

After they were out of hearing, the General began:
" Well, sir, did you see that beautiful young lady that
passed through our lines to-day ?"

" I saw several ladies; you must be more specific," said
Virtus, with a crimson blush. " I refer to a young lady
riding a gay black horse, accompanied by two servants."

" Yes, sir; I saw her—and a fine looking lady she is."

" Did you ever see her before ?"

" My impression is that I have."

All this time the General had been looking quisically
into our heroe's eyes, as if to read the feeling of his soul.

" Will you pardon me for asking you, where you think
you saw her ?"

" At —— station, sir, if I am not mistaken."

" When ?"

" When we passed through that place en route to ——
city, to form your regiment."

" Precisely; and unless I am mistaken, the boys had a
laugh on you about her."

" I believe they did, sir."

" It is not my purpose to pry into your secrets; yet,
my friendship for you, my admiration for her, and the
rather remarkable circumstance which gave rise to the
innocent sport at your expense, which the boys indulged
in on the occasion just alluded to—all this, I say, has
awakened in me an interest in your behalf."

"Thank you, sir; but how did your 'admiration of the lady' become so soon excited?"

"I happened to meet her in the road to-day, and had a long conversation with her. She is at once the most beautiful, intelligent, and accomplished young lady, I think, I ever saw. They are escaping from the yankees, and going a few miles below, to a relation's house. If I can assist you in any way, I am at your service."

"Thank you, General; I may call on you soon. I wish, at least, to form her acquaintance; and I would be glad, if duty should not conflict, to have the privilege of visiting the family next Thursday."

"You shall, certainly, unless something serious should transpire, have the privilege of visiting them; and, as the old lady invited me down on the same day, I hope to be able to accompany you."

"Every thing seems to work well," thought Virtus, as he expressed his thanks to the General for his kindness.

"But this is not all I wish to speak to you about. I have received an order from Major General M— to appear with my brigade to-morrow, at 10 o'clock, a. m. [Sunday], for the purpose of brigade review. Now, I am at a loss to know what to do. Shall I obey the order, or not?"

"The Army Regulations do not *require* such exercises on the Sabbath; and there is no pressing *necessity* for such review. Besides, it would tend to destroy the services of the Sabbath, cause the irreligious to disregard the day, and the army gradually to become a pandemonium. For my part, I will say that, if I ever *have* to do such a thing on the Sabbath, it will be done *under protest;* so that the sin of desecrating the Lord's day will be chargeable, not to *me,* but to *him* who extorts obedience to his unrighteous demands.

I am fully aware, also, that there is an oath administered to us all *to obey our superior officers;* yet it was, of course, understood that their orders would not be such as to confiict with our obligations to God. Should an officer command me to plaspheme the name of God, or to take my own life, it would be sinful in me to obey him. And, if I am ordered to violate any of the laws of God, I shall prefer to 'obey God rather than man.'

"But you ask me whether you shall obey the order. This you must decide for yourself. I should first write a polite note, informing the Major General that there are no army regulations requiring such an exercise on the Sabbath, that you and many of your brigade are religiously opposed to such desecration of the Sabbath, and that, therefore, you hope he will revoke the order."

"This is just what I have written, only that I have dressed the matter up in a little milder language. I am anxiously awaiting a reply. Here comes the messenger now."

The note was handed to Gen. B—, and he read as follows:

"Brig. Gen. B—: My order is unrevoked—appear on the field at the hour appointed.

Major General M—."

Now came the "tug of war," more disagreeable by far than fighting the yankees.

He took up a piece of paper, and wrote thus:

"Major Gen. M—: Sir, I regret that you have not revoked your order; for I cannot, without doing violence to my conscience, obey it; and it would be pleasant to die, in preference to doing this. If you choose, I will consider myself under arrest, and will gladly appear before a court-martial, to answer for my conduct. Very respectfully, &c.,

"Brig. Gen. B."

When the Major General read this note he felt very angry, and determined to arrest the man that was so presumptuous as to disregard his orders; but after reflection led him to pursue a different course. He felt convinced the offender would be acquitted before a court-martial, or,

6

if not, that the matter would be referred to the government authorities, where, he felt sure. the decision would go against him. Not, therefore, through any regard for the Sabbath, or kind feelings towards the offender, but for fear of losing his case, and subjecting himself to the criticism of the pious, generally, he sent back the following note :

Brig. Gen. B—, Not wishing to have an open eruption with you, I suppose, in this instance, I shall have to respect your weakness. You need not appear for drill at 10, a. m., to-morrow.

Maj. Gen. M."

The messenger returned, and Gen. B— and Virtus were left alone together.

"I am glad the matter has resulted thus," said Virtus; "yet it might have been better for our armies, generally, if it had been referred to Congress; for, had the question been pressed upon that body for a decision, there is little ground to doubt that they would have placed their veto upon such wanton desecration of the Sabbath. But, for your sake, I am glad it is settled."

"It is," said the general, "very strange that our authorities did not regulate this matter at first. How it could have been left arbitrary with generals to desecrate the Sabbath, and cause, at will, thousands of pious soldiers to spend the day in drills, reviews, inspections, &c., is beyond my comprehension."

After the conversation on this subject closed, Gen. B— asked Virtus this question :

"How can I exert the best influence over the men under my charge—officers and privates ?"

"In the first place, being a Christian yourself, you should 'let your light shine' conspicuously before all. More than this, you should use your position so as to promote the influence of your teachings Then, secondly. Encourage Chaplains to persevere in their labor; urge Christians to do their whole duty; warn sinners to forsake their sins. Encourage your men to bear, like good soldiers, the burdens, hardships, and dangers of war, tempering firmness with kindness. Thirdly.—Teach every officer and private his duty to his country, to himself, and to his God. Suppress all gross immoralities, such as profanity, intoxication, card-playing, stealing, &c. Finally.—*See to it that every man treats every other* in a proper way. Let no officer abuse a private, or private insult an officer, with impunity.

" Do all this, and you will have the happiness of knowing that yours is one of the most efficient brigades in the service ; do this, and you will be the means of saving the morals of many a soldier, if not his soul; do this, and you will have a conscience void of offence towards God and man ; do this, and you will deserve the profound gratitude of all the good in your brigade, of many wives, mothers, and sisters, and of posterity ; do this, and when you gain admittance through the pearly gates of the New Jerusalem, many a star will glisten in your crown of rejoicing."

With profound interest did the general listen to all that our hero said ; and his serious look showed how deeply he felt a sense of his responsibility. Thanking his adviser for his counsel, he said :

'" I must adopt system in my labors, else little will be done."

" Yes," said the other, " system is the key to success. Without it, we have little time for any thing; with it, we can do a great deal, and have much time to spare.

" I would advise you to assemble your whole brigade, at least once a week, for the purpose of impressing upon all the importance of adopting system, and give them such other advice as will enable them to see their responsibility, and make the best of their time possible."

" I will do it," responded the general.

" By doing so you will add much to the pleasure, as well as to the good, of the brigade. The men will, I think, be delighted to know that their leader is so deeply interested in their behalf. Nothing helps one so much as to know that his superiors are interested in and desire his good."

" Very true," replied the general; "and I am surprised that this idea had not occurred to me before. Why did you not mention it to me ?"

" I have thought of doing so a number of times, but have been waiting for a suitable opportunity. I do not wish to make myself too officious, because you are disposed to regard me kindly."

" Do not allow such ideas to enter your head. I esteem your friendship too highly, not to regard properly your actions. But what time in the week would it be most likely to please the men to meet ? I want to consult their convenience ; for on that, to a considerable extent, at least, depends their appreciation of this."

" That, of course, will depend on circumstances. When we are stationed—as we are now—almost any evening could be chosen."

" This, I believe, is Saturday."

" Yes."

" Then to-morrow I will announce a meeting for next Friday evening, If nothing more than I know of should occur."

" I shall be very glad to hear your lectures on the proposed subjects, and can only hope that duty will not deprive me of the pleasure of hearing the first," replied Virtus.

" If you would only consent to receive a position, my dear friend, that would place you more at liberty, I would be most happy."

To this our hero merely replied :

" We have sufficiently discussed that matter before."

As it was growing late, the private retired to his own

tent, there to seek that repose which is so sweet to the
weary when a consciousness of having performed faithfully
the duties of the day, abides with him. This night, however, though at rest in conscience, and weary of body, Virtus could not easily compose himself to sleep. And when
at last the drowsy god asserted his power, dreams of a certain
lovely face and form visited and flitted through the mind
of the sleeper.

The Sabbath was beautifully mild and calm. Anxious
listeners gathered together under the branches of the
spreading forest to hear the word of God expounded.
Officers and men knelt under nature's temple, to return
grateful thanks to the "Giver of all Good."

It was a noteworthy fact that, though no man was com-
pelled to attend Divine service, there were few of the general's old regiment absent from the assembly of anxious
worshipers. It will never be known in this world how
much influence for good a pious, consistent general may
exert over the men whom he commands; nor how much
influence for evil an ungodly, tyrannical general may exert
over his men. Their responsibility is fearful!

But let us return to the service.

Our noble Chaplain, after singing and prayer, announced
the following as his text:

"*I am not ashamed of the Gospel of Christ; for it is the
power of God unto salvation to every one that believeth.*"

"Well," said the distinguished speaker, "might the
Apostle make the declaration, 'I am not ashamed of the
Gospel of Christ,' while he had so good a reason to support his position. Men ought to be ashamed of many
positions which they assume, because they have no *good*
reason to sustain them; but while '*salvation* is the legiti-
mate reason for any position assumed, no one need be
ashamed of that position. *Why?* Because it is the *best*
and, therefore, the *strongest* reason that man can assign for
his conduct or opinions.

"*Salvation!* What does it imply? It implies that, without the Gospel man is *lost*—lost forever—banished from the presence of God and angels—left to endure the penal consequences due to his multiplied transgressions. To the lost soul, no ray of joy, peace, or hope can ever penetrate! Eternal misery, 'the gnawings of the worm that never dies,' must be the portion of the poor, lost soul!

"But 'salvation' implies release from this awful state. Nor is this all: It implies a well-grounded hope of admittance into the blessed city. It furnishes 'unspeakable joy' here, and eternal blessedness hereafter.

"'The spirits of just men made perfect,' the angels of God, and Christ himself, will be the associates of the *saved* soul

"Release from *infinite torture*, and the enjoyment of *infinite bliss*, are the results of '*salvation.*' Now, what can be more desirable than to escape the *one*, and obtain the *other?* The Apostle's reason, therefore, is two-fold: 1st. to escape eternal punishment; and, 2d. To obtain eternal blessedness.

"Who, then, would be ashamed of that which brings such important results? Who would be ashamed of the Gospel of Christ? Who would be ashamed of Him Who, by His incarnation, obedience, suffering, death, and resurrection, made it possible for man to obtain a seat in the New Jerusalem.

"But *how* is man to avail himself of the benefits of Christ's atonement? By *believing*. The Gospel of Christ is the power of God to every one that '*believeth.*' Believeth what? Believeth the Gospel of Christ. Will *you* not all believe this precious Gospel? Why not?"

I have given nothing more than the general outlies of the sermon: to appreciate, fully, it was necessary to *hear* it, and *see* the speaker.

At the close of the sermon, the general arose, made a touching appeal to the men to seek salvation, and announced his purpose of delivering a series of lectures on certain subjects, beginning next Friday evening.

After prayer and singing, the congregation was dismissed.

It is proper to state, that the other troops encamped near this brigade were, while Gen. B—'s men were enjoying religious service, engaged in making a great "military display."

What a contrast! *Here* praises ascended to Him Who giveth the victory to Whom He will; *there* the holy Sabbath was openly, and without reason, desecrated!

Why Gen. B—'s brigade was not present at the "grand review," his own men, except a very few, did not know; but they thought they knew enough of the general to know that he would resign any military position before he would wantonly violate the Sabbath. And in this they had judged him correctly; for he had resolved that, rather than disregard the Sabbath, he would throw up his commission, and fight as a private.

His men, in view of their belief that their general had resolved not to desecrate the Lord's day, had their appreciation of him much heightened. Proud they were to serve under such a noble and devotedly pious man.

Every thing went on smoothly till Thursday morning, the day agreed upon to visit the family, important members of which the general and our hero had already seen. So meeting Virtus early after breakfast, the general said to him, "Will you be ready after morning drill, to pay these ladies our contemplated visit?"

"Yes, sir; at least I know of nothing to prevent. I will be at your service early after drill."

"We will leave at half-past ten o'clock, a. m.," said the general. "Come up to my head-quarters," continued he, "and you shall ride our noble black, that has carried you safely through a more dangerous expedition."

" Thank you, general, was the modest reply of the noble youth.

According to promise, Virtus appeared at the general's head-quarters, dressed in his best suit, which was made of gray Confederate jeans, with the necessary sprinkling of brass buttons. It is not my design to describe his manly appearance on the occasion; suffice it, that he had no cause to blush, and the truly refined could but admire him.

They were soon on their way. The general was unusually mirthful, while his companion was almost silent.

Our hero could only command sufficient control over himself to pay that regard to his officer's mood which was required of him. He would gladly have ridden in silence, but he knew such a course would not only be disrespectful to Gen. B—, but would also bring upon himself raillery; for no one enjoyed jesting more than Gen. B—.

After a few miles' ride they entered the beautiful grounds of ————. All the surroundings showed that abundant wealth was possessed by the owners.

" This is a splendid place," remarked the general; " and we may safely promise ourselves a pleasant evening, if the family is as well cultivated as the grounds."

" That they are, those who have seen and conversed with them cannot doubt," was the gallant reply.

" On the defensive already, are you? I shall have to use caution in your presence. One who can learn so much from one or two chance meetings, and consider it his duty to play the defender, may prove dangerous."

" Not at all, General: but you must yourself admit that Miss ———— is a lady of refinement," was the blushing reply.

" Well, yes; I was rather impressed with that fact.— But yonder comes that little rogue, whose birthday we are to celebrate."

Little Kate, in her joy and eagerness, ran and opened the gate before a servant could be summoned.

"I am so glad to see you," she exclaimed, while they were dismounting. "Just think of having a general at my candy-pulling! It makes me quite proud. And I am just as glad to have you, too," said she, turning to Virtus. Then, as naturally as if they had been old friends, she held up her rosy mouth for a kiss from each. Entering into a playful conversation with the merry child, they walked up the broad graveled walk to the piaza, where they were met and most cordially welcomed by the gentlemen and old Mrs. Morton.

They were ushered immediately into the spacious parlor, where Virtus was formally introduced to the one who had been seen in many a dream. He could not keep down a flashing color; nor did he fail to notice the "rosy blushes" that bloomed in Miss Lula Love's cheeks. The presentation of the saucy school-girl, Lina, was quite a relief.

Taking in all, it was quite a happy gathering. The merry Kate was allowed to do as she pleased, and it pleased her to have all attention. No one must refuse to join in her amusement. Even Gen. B— had to consent to engage in a game of "club fist."

Mixing in this child's play, any restraint that might have been felt at first, soon passed away. Not many hours elapsed before *strangeness* wore off, and each felt the feeling of friend to friend, except, perhaps, Virtus and Miss Lula. While each seemed to look upon the other indifferently, a close observer could not fail to detect the interest they felt. They spoke to each other unrestrainedly on many subjects, and every thing caused them to look more intently within, at the feelings springing into existence.

Long before the visit was over, Virtus had resolved to seek, and, if possible, win the hand and heart of the charming lady, provided further acquaintance did not lessen his admiration; and there was little doubt in his mind in regard to this subject.

During the day, General B—— took occasion, when old

Mrs. Morton had made some complimentary remark about his friend, to relate in detail much of his gallant conduct; and also to speak in the highest terms of his family connection. This very much gratified the old lady, who complacently remarked:

"I knew he was a *gentleman*, when I first saw him. No mean man can look as he does."

It is but proper to state that the young people had strayed out into the beautiful grounds, before this conversation commenced. Our hero would never have allowed himself to be made conspicuous, had he been present.

Meantime Virtus is delighted with the sensible and beautiful remarks made by Miss Lula. He very gradually led the conversation to the discussion of what is requisite to constitute a happy married life.

"In the first place," said Miss Lula, "the parties entering upon this state ought to assure themselves that their dispositions are congenial."

"Certainly," said Virtus, "for without congeniality, *love* cannot exist; and without that mutual love which enables each to *bear* and *forbear*, nothing but misery can be expected. A thorough knwledge of the character, hence, should be obtained by all who enter this state. May this be considered another requisite?"

"It may; and to obtain this knowledge an acquaintance of time is required," was the reply.

"True. But may not the time be short?"

"Under some circumstances it might. But such cases do not, I think, occur often. Time *will* show faults, and if all lovers would wait for *blindness* to pass away, there would be fewer unhappy marriages."

"I agree with you, in thinking that the *blindness* should pass away; or rather, I do not think the *purest* and *best* love blinds us. Where *judgment* and *reason* can perceive those qualities which, we know, are necessary to happiness, an *appreciation* arises which is far above what is commonly regarded as love. If judgment and reason do not recommend a union, it seems to me to be folly in any one to marry."

" Yes, but your *judges*—judgment and reason—are often very stern."

" But not the less just."

" True, but who would choose a wife or a husband, merely regarding them ? While their decisions ought never to be violated, I am far from believing that nothing else is necessary. Affection should be taken into the account too, else matrimony becomes a mere business transaction, and every one with nice feelings objects to bartering away himself."

" I see," said Virtus, " we will be quibbling about terms. You use '*feelings*,' '*love*,' in the sense I do *appreciation*. Well then, when *love, reason* and *judgment* coincide, all may be considered right."

" Provided the *acquaintance* is sufficient to furnish the real traits in the characters of each."

" That reminds me," said Virtus, " that we may often know the character of persons, without having any, or a very limited personal acquaintance with them. Might not love spring up under such circumstances ?"

" Possibly. But it is more usually admiration in such cases. We may admire, where love would be impossible."

" Suppose two persons should be mutually attracted toward each other upon their first meeting, may the resulting feeling be regarded a good basis for matrimony ?" inquired our hero, while a blush suffused the cheek of either.

After a moment's hesitation Miss Lula replied :

" That, I suppose, more properly comes under the head of admiration, which may deepen into love in time. *To love*, without having some ground wherein to exercise *judgment* and *reason*, must appear very silly to you," she replied laughingly.

Virtus laughed too, and blushed as he thought of the admiration his lovely companion called forth the first time he ever saw her. He seemed to have forgotton what they were conversing about, for he abruptly asked: " What do you think of love at first sight? Is it not, after all about as reliable a test as persons could be governed by ?"

" I thought," said Miss Lula, " that we had already agreed that *reason* should be allowed to act her part in the matter. And if this be so, then it is certain that time would be necessry in order for reason to collect facts, and make up her judgment."

"This is all very well; yet it does not reach the principle after which I was inquiring. Love, I take it, is nothing more than that agreeable feeling which springs up in the minds of congenial spirits, when they are brought within the sphere of attraction. Where this feeling springs up mutually between a couple, reason, unless the parties belong to the stoics, has little power or disposition to search after blemishes, while it serves as a magnifying glass through which all the virtues of the *loved* one are favorably exaggerated. Moreover, would nature allow mutual love to spring up, where the parties are ill suited to each other ?"

Too much under the influence of the sacred flame, to deny its power, or to speak lightly of it, the maiden, with crimson checks, replied: " Granting that all you say is true, it would certainly tend but to heighten love, if, as you say is usually the case, reason adds the force of her decision to the noble feeling of love. Besides, it seems to be an axiom with me, that before one is wedded to another for life, the parties should both *know* what they are doing."

While this conversation was going on, they were both unconsciously plucking flowers, and each, by this time, had quite a handful. Their conversation was interrupted by the ringing of the dinner bell.

" Let us walk in to dinner," said the lovely Lula, gazing modestly into the soldier's face. While on the way to the house, such thoughts as these fluttered through her mind :

" *Why* is it that this soldier has stolen my affections—why should those tender emotions of which I hitherto supposed myself incapable, spring into existence at the sight of a stranger? Noble man that he is! How brilliant his intellect, how refined his feelings, how noble his heart, and how acute his sense of honor and propriety! Such a man is worthy the affections of a better woman than I am!"

Thus it is that love views only the virtues of the one around whom the affections are entwined; while the lover, magnifying the excellencies of the *loved* one, imagines himself or herself unworthy of the affections of the one enshrined in the heart. But though this, in many cases, is true; I presume it has never yet happened that a lover was willing to take the logical consequences of this sense of unworthiness—viz; reject the hand of the one deemed so much superior.

Seated at the dinner table, the General, partly to tease Virtus, and partly to amuse the dinner party, turning to our hero, said : " A soldier's life would be comparatively happy, if he could have the pleasure of enjoying the society of ladies, would it not ?"

" It is quite a treat, General, for the soldier, accustomed to naught but soldiers' society, to be allowed the pleasure of mingling with ladies."

Upon this, Miss Lula's face caught a sublime crimson glow, while Virtus, with all his self-possession, could not dare for a moment to turn his eyes from his plate.

The conversation was carried on very pleasantly during the feast, and immediately on retiring from the table, the General looking at his watch, exclaimed, " It is now full time we were in camps !"

These words were anything but pleasant to all the party, young and old, especially to Miss Lula and Virtus.

" I regret," said Mrs. Morton, " that you cannot spend the evening with us."

" Under other circumstances, it would afford us (mean-

ing Virtus and himself) much pleasure to do so; but ' duty
before pleasure,' you know, should be a governing principle with us."

"Certainly; but you must both call again soon—we will
be happy to see you," said the kind lady of the house; and
in this sentiment all the family were agreed.

"Thank you, madam," replied the general; "it will afford us much pleasure to call again soon, if duty will allow;" and with this, they bade the kind people adieu, not,
however, until Virtus had received a kind of side invitation from Miss Lula, to call again, which, of course, he un-
reluctantly agreed to do.

They had scarcely cleared the gate, when the general began: "Well, Virtus, I hope you have had a fine time of
it; you and that young Miss seemed to enjoy yourselves
admirably."

"A very fine time, sir; it is quite a green spot in a soldier's life, to be permitted to while away an hour with such
a family."

"And with such a *young lady*, especially," added the
general.

"I accept the emphasis, General; and confess that Miss
Lula is quite a nice young lady."

"Not quite so cold and self-possessed," exclaimed the
general, with a broad smile on his face. "You had as well
own up at once; for that you and Miss Lula are both tre-
mendously involved in love, is too plain for a man with one
eye not to see. Come, now, make me your confident, and
I will help you through, if you should need any assistance."

"Well, General, I must say that I have a very great
admiration for Miss Lula; so much so, that I have a desire
to see her again; and, of course, I am very much obliged
to you for your proffered aid."

"Whenever duty will allow, you can have leave of absence," said the general, laughingly.

"I thank you, sir; I will, if duty will allow, avail myself of your kind permission."

Thus they talked till they came within the lines of the encampment, when other matters attracted the officer's attention,; and though the private had other things to employ his body, he found it difficult to disengage his mind from her who, to tell plain truth, had stolen his heart.

But let us listen to what was said by the family with whom they had dined:

"Very pleasant gentlemen." said old Mrs. Morton to her daughter.

"Yes," replied the other, "I have rarely seen two more interesting gentlemen. And what is remarkable, their different ranks seem to form not the least barrier in their way—the general seems to think as much of the private, as if both were of the same grade in office."

"Yes, and well he may, in this case," exclaimed Mrs. Morton; "for, from the general's own account, that private is quite his equal intellectually; his superior, morally; and not inferior to any one, in true bravery."

"Did the general tell you much about him?"

"Yes; he spent at least an hour in telling of what the private has done, and of the noble character he possesses; as also of his family. More than this, he says that the young man persistently declines any office, and that his reasons for doing so are so strong, that the general himself cannot answer them. The general thinks he has no equal, if he is a private."

"Give us his history, if it is so interesting."

The old lady then, in a conversation of about two hours, detailed the incidents in the character of our hero, which the General had related to her. Nor was Miss Lula, though all the time silent,. an inattentive listener. She eagerly, though apparently in a listless mood, drank down every word—storing up carefully every feat performed, and treasuring up every virtue that was displayed in the conduct

of our noble hero. Now it was that the decisions of reason blended most happily with the strong emotions of love
which had, from the first sight, so strongly sprung up in
her heart, and which, despite herself, so often painted her
cheeks with the hues of the scarlet rose. It may be
enough, for the present, to say, that they both loved with
their first affections, and that their reason sanctioned this
noble exercise of the soul.

Little of note transpired in camp, till the time arrived
for the General's first lecture. It will be impossible for
me to lay before the reader anything more than a brief out-
line of these admirable discourses. Would that every
General had the capacity and will to deliver such lectures
to his men; then would the tented field appear as a Bethel,
and the term of service would be one of great advantage
to the large majority of our brave soldiers.

But to the lectures.

The first was delivered on the subject: " *My duty to
myself.*"

After a touching introduction, the dignified speaker
elaborated the following propositions :

" 1. I owe it to myself to preserve my health. To do
this, it is necessary for me to keep my person *clean*, to
observe regular habits in eating, sleeping, and exercise.
Every needless violation of the laws of health, forfeits
one's right to health, if not to life. Cleanliness and taste
in dress we owe both to ourselves and to our associates.

" 2. We owe it to ourselves to improve our manners.
If we are disposed, we can, as easily as not, be polite and
agreeable. The dignity of the human species requires us
all to make ourselves as affable and agreeable as possible,
without acquiring a disgusting affectation.

" 3. We owe it to ourselves to improve our intellects.
Knowledge is very much to the intellect what food is to
the body : It imparts vigor, strength and polish to it.

" Situated as we are, without books, we cannot acquire

knowledge as rapidly as we might do if at home ; yet we have ample opportunities to study ' nature, principles and things.' And if we will but improve our time properly, we may add daily to our stock of knowledge, and thereby polish our intellects more and more.

"4. We owe it to ourselves to cultivate our moral principles, and refine all our feelings.

"To be successful in this, we must never gratify any of the mean desires and appetites in our nature. We must never cherish an impure thought or desire, speak an unchaste word, or commit a mean, base or doubtful action. For if we do either of these, we degrade the spiritual man, —we impose a foul stain upon our souls, which rivers of tears will never be able to wash out; nor can an after life of virtue atone for the infamy thus induced. The Bible says, "As a man thinketh, so is he." Impurity of life begins in impure thoughts; impure thoughts often excite impure desires, and impure desires often result in base, degrading actions. Hence, we should discard all impure thoughts, and cherish naught but such thoughts as will elevate and refine us. Let us cultivate pure imaginations —establish a lofty ideal of honor, integrity, and virtue; nor let us ever be content until we have made the highest possible attainments in all these excellences.

"Finally. We owe it to ourselves to secure, pure and undefied religion.

"Without this, every other possible attainment will fail to make us happy. The gulf between the sinner's soul and happiness, is impassable by any virtue of his own. Man by nature is *lost*—lost to holiness, happiness and to the favor of God. These can be secured only by ' repentance towards God, and faith in the Lord Jesus Christ. It is the duty of each sinner to repent of his sins, and accept of Christ as his Savior. You cannot afford to postpone this matter. '*Now is the day of salvation.*'"

There is no means of estimating the amount of good that

7

resulted from this lecture.   It made a lasting impression on
t'ie minds of many.

Before the time for the next lecture, the General in command ordered a reconnoisance to be made in the direction
of the enemy ; and a requisition was made upon Gen. B—
for some men, of unquestioned valor and ability, as they
would be required to go far within the supposed lines of
the enemy.   It is needless to say that Virtus was one of
the number selected for this hazardous mission.

Mounted on fleet chargers, those appointed to make the
reconnoisance, started in the direction of the enemy.   They
had proceeded but a few miles, when crowds of refugees—
old men, women and children—met them.   They all seemed
delighted at seeing Confederate Soldiers ; and gave uni-
form testimony of the brutal treatment the Federals were
giving our citizens.   Robbery and incendiarism marked
the advance of the enemy !   Modern warfare furnishes no
example of a people, so heartless and unprincipled, as the
hypoc:itical, puritanical Yankees !

The scouting party now reached the town near which
Miss Lula Love once resided.   The stately mansion which
she *once* called home, was now lonely and desolate.   A few
old servants, tried and true, were left to take care, as best
they could, of the noble residence.   No earthly house
presented such attractions to Virtus.   Even the birds that
sang so sadly in the richly decorated bower in front of the
house, seemed to touch, with their plaintive melodies, all
the solemn chords in his heart.   An ardent love, tempered
with sadness by the calamities brought upon the family,
and indignation at the miserable, heartless robbers who oc-
casioned all this sadness—these, with a firm resolve to .
avenge the wrong, were his prominent feelings while passing the once happy abode of the loved Lula.   Fain would
he have stopped to gaze upon the flower-yard, made beautiful by the hands of the fair maiden, but *duty* allowed no
delay.

They had not gone more than six miles farther, when
the Yankee vanguard appeared in the distance. The party,
unobserved, fell back a few hundred yards, left the road,
and ascended a high hill, from which point they could easily
see all the forces of the enemy as they passed   From this
stand point, our hero counted thirty-two regiments of infantry, four batteries of 8 guns each, and two regiments of
cavalry. They also counted the number of men, as accu-
rately as they could, in several of the regiments; and decided that the regiments would average about 525 men,
each. So that the whole force numbered between 18,000
and 19,000 men. After the enemy had all passed except
a few stragglers, the party descended to the road and captured a few prisoners, from whom they learned that the
entire Yankee corps had passed.

All the desired information had now been acquired,
touching the number and movements of the enemy, but
" how shall we convey this to head-quarters?" was a question of great moment. Our hero knew of but one road
that would lead him back to his command; and it would
not do to think of travelling this. To make their way
through the woods and fields was their only alternative, and
thus they began their rough journey, traveling much of
the time within sight of the road, which was filled with
Yankees. As they drew near the town through which
they had passed in the morning, Virtus had tha unspeakable mortification of seeing the princely residence of Miss
Lula wrapt in flames! "There is a day of retribution
ahead!" lowly muttered the hero. " I will never ask for a
furlough, while a Yankee foot presses Southern soil!"

The enemy had thrown out pickets all around the village,
which they were now plundering; and lucky would he be,
who could pass within sight of the town without being
seen. Such good fortune did not fall to the lot of our gallant
party; for, not far before them, were clearly visible not
less than a dozen pickets! These, however, were easily

avoided by a hasty and remote "flank movement." One
hill was descended, another ascended, and our brave boys
were out of danger for the present at least.

Moving on in a direction parallel with the road, our little
party had gone about four miles when they came to a road
that evidently led into the one that would guide them to
camps; but pickets, our model soldier rightly thought,
were posted at the junction of the two roads. Hence the
former road was crossed. and the forest, dense though it
was. must be explored.

They had but passed through this skirt of woods, when
they came within full view of a Yankee regiment of cavalry,
encamped in a grove near a large cornfield, into which they
had turned their horses. Wheeling to run, the enemy saw
our scouts, and began to make every effort to pursue them.

Though most of the enemy's horses were loose in the
field, yet some of them were saddled, and ready for the
chase. Probably about 160 were sent in pursuit, some immediately towards our little band, and others on ahead, so
as to cut them off. The prospect for their escape was
indeed gloomy! Yet if they were to be captured, the
prize would be estimated. if for no other reason, because it
would be so costly to the captors.

Not many minutes had elapsed before it became
evident that the pursued must wheel and fight. Gaining
a favorable position, they halted, but not to surrender as
the pursuers supposed; for, of the ten Yankees who were
nearest at hand. eight were seen to fall from their saddles,
on the reception of the first volley. The other two
"changed their base." by retreating as rapidly as possible.
The firing attracted the other pursuers, but when they came
near enough to hear the screams of their wounded comrades,
our horses were several hundred yards from them, so that
escape now seemed possible.

As they turned to go down a long sloping hill, they discovered a squad of Yankees on before them to the right,

a number about equal to their own. On seeing the Confederates the vandals halted, and began to look around, as if to count their own strength. Seeing which, our gallants dashed towards them, and they fled in wild confusion toward their encampment; but not every one by several, were fortunate enough to escape.

Virtus with his little band now galloped on in the direction of their camps, and saw nothing more of the enemy that evening. An hour more, and our noble hero reported to Gen. B——. The general was very much delighted at the success of the reconnoisance, and went to report immediately to the General in command; who, on learning that the reconnoitering party was commanded by a *private*, was very much displeased; but when Gen. B— told him of the character of Virtus, asserting that the private was the most reliable man, for such service, in his brigade, the old General gave way, and expressed himself as satisfied. Yet the glowing discription given of our hero, caused even this austere old General, who was wont to estimate a soldier merely on the basis of *rank*, to express a desire to see this " remarkable private."

" I would be pleased," said Gen. B—, " to introduce him to you. I am sure you would admire him. He is one of the most intellectual, pure, incorruptible and gentlemanly men I ever knew. Most men would consider him eccentric, but when you probe his eccentrity to the bottom, you find it to be an extraordinary attachment to principle—principle of the right kind."

" Send for him to come here," said the other; "I wish to *test* him."

Virtus was sent for, and quickly made his appearance.

" Allow me," said Gen. B— " to present you with my friend, Private Virtus, General —— ——.' Our hero bowed gracefully, while the officer was far more polite than was his custom to privates. The General then asked him to narrate the particulars of his reconnoisance. This the hero did in a concise, intelligent and unembarrassed manner. The old General was much delighted with the young man, and. wishing to make our hero's talent available, said, " I would be pleased to attach you to my staff," at the same time tendering him a position with the rank of Lieutenant.

" I am much obliged to you, Sir; but it is my resolve to serve my country as best I can, as a private."

The old General raised his head in astonishment! "What! refuse to be an officer! I never heard of such a thing! Have you any *reason* for this?"

" I think I have, sir."

Our hero then proceeded to state all his reasons in order, and invited the General to answer them. But this he was not able to do. Near the close of the conversation, the General, in a very complimentary way, told Virtus that he might consider himself the chief of all important reconnoitering parties; to which he replied: " I am always ready to do all I can to serve my country."

Excitement and expectation prevailed throughout the encampment, when it become generally known that double their number of the enemy were so near. The over brave were desirous of making an immediate attack on the enemy, but the General in command considered " discretion the better part of valor," and the failure of the expected reinforcements to arrive determined him to "retreat." Ere the morning light broke, the tents had been "struck," and the encampment deserted. Much to the honor of the commanding officer, but little was left for the vandals to glory over. Every bridge was burned in the rear, and many obstructions placed in the enemy's way, should they continue to advance.

Upon inquiry, Virtus found that the main body of troops would not pass the residence of Lula's uncle, as it was about two miles from the most direct road. Thought he : " What plan can I devise to inform this interesting family of our retreat? It is possible for them not to know soon enough to make their escape. The lovely Lula must be warned. I must make the effort to see her once more too."

With such thoughts as these, he sought Gen. B—, whom he found just ready to leave. After hearing Virtus he said :

" You are more thoughtful than I am. Amid so many duties, I had forgotten those friends. Yes, they must have warning in time. They have done too much for our cause not to escape the brutality of the Federals. But whom will we send round to tell them ?"

"If you do not object, that would be a pleasant duty for me to perform," was the modest reply.

Though weightier matters weighed on his mind, Gen. B— could not restrain a smile at this reply,

" I can imagine your anxiety, considering the fair Lula." said he; "and suppose you must have the privilege of seeing her again, though I would much like to have you with me. Good scouting leaders will be much needed."

" With your permission, General, I will not think of the last part of your speech, but interpret the former in my favor. As for scouting leaders, you can find enough."

" O you must go, I see. Well, present my kindest regards to the family, but do not allow stronger than Yankee chains to bind you."

" Thank you! I will be up with the command before noon."

" You ride, of course : to undertake such a trip on foot must not be thought of."

" I am an *infantry* private ; and only ride when on certain important duty," was the reply.

" But is there no horse you can get? I am sorry I have none to offer you. To go so far out of the way, and then overtake the troops, will be very fatiguing," said the General, uneasily.

" I could gladly ' double-quick' the whole distance, rather than to miss conveying such important information. The wagons are, I believe, all gone, and the horses with them. I shall get along very well on foot, never fear."

"The attractions of Miss Lula must indeed be highly appreciated, to tempt you to do this."

"It would be unkind, general, to leave that warm-hearted Southern family to fall into the enemy's hands," said Virtus."

"Yes; and I leave you to warn them of the impending danger; but do not linger too long. You may be needed elsewhere;" saying which, Gen. B— rode off, and Virtus joyfully set out to perform his self-imposed task.

"I must," said he, "make all possible speed, so that *they* can leave before the troops pass."

He pressed eagerly forward, and soon after daylight entered the grounds of Mr.—.

He met old Mrs. Morton on the piazza. The busy old lady was delighted and surprised to see him at that early hour. A few hasty inquiries were indulged in, and she hastened to arouse the gentlemen, who were addicted to taking morning naps. Soon the entire family were up, and hasty preparations commenced for their flight. Our hero enjoyed half an hour's *tete-a-tete* with Miss Lula, despite the general excitement.

Immediately after breakfast, Virtus arose, and commenced bidding the family adieu, when Mr. Morton said:

"Can you not wait until we are ready to go? Your company will be very acceptable."

"Thank you, I would be much pleased to do as you suggest, but must overtake the command as soon as possible. I fear I have already tarried longer than is consistent with duty."

"You must not, of course, neglect duty, in order to gratify us. Run, Katy, and call a servant to bring the gentleman's horse round."

"Do not trouble yourself," said Virtus, "I belong to the infantry."

"Yes, but you certainly did not come so far out of your way on foot to serve us?"

"I could not get a horse, but was too willing to warn you, to allow such a trifle to be a hindrance."

"You must leave a-foot, then. Our cause of gratitude was sufficient before this was known, but it is heightened now," said old Mrs. Morton; and she was warmly seconded by the other members of the family, Miss Lula not excepted.

Virtus felt somewhat embarrassed by the commendations, and thanks showered upon him, but retained enough of composure to reply:

"I do not deserve any thanks for this simple, humane act. To have served you is a sufficient reward. A few miles walk is of but little importance to one accustomed to marching. I hope you will all be able to get away from the federals. And now, I really must be going."

"Wait a moment," said Mrs. Love, "the buggy will soon be around; and I will ask you to take one of the girls to the hotel at ——. Thus, you will oblige me, and save yourself so long a walk."

If such an arrangement will favor you in the slightest, I will be happy to oblige you," said Virtus, devoutly hoping that Miss Lula's company would be his just a little longer.

"It will oblige me, for Lina cannot drive. Lula has a sore hand, and one of them must go in the buggy. Come, girls, which one of you can get ready soonest? Mr. Virtus is anxious to be off; so don't keep him waiting."

"O, Pa, I cannot be ready these two hours, for my worsted work is all unpacked, and I must not lose that," said Lina, as her father's eye rested on her.

"And you would almost as soon lose yourself as your worsted work! Then, Lula, can you be ready soon?"

"In a very few minutes," said she, while a crimson blush grew into her cheeks.

Virtus, it is needless to say, was highly gratified at this happy arrangement. The hotel referred to, was a short distance beyond the position the army would occupy, but he agreed that he could take Miss Lula there, and get back to his command by noon.

Very soon, Miss Lula, looking very lovely in her dark riding dress, reported herself ready to go. Though every thing on their way was in confusion, the ride was not without its pleasures. In fact, the blind god had already put it into the heart of Virtus to exercise unlimited belief in Lula's perfections; and he felt that to be near her, to see her gentle smile, to hear her sweet words, was sufficient cause of happiness. Still his reason forbade his speaking a word of love, yet the eye, as is often the case, performed the office of the reluctant tongue.

Both knew that they loved and *were* loved—that was sufficient. Time would bring the lip confession.

Our hero succeeded in placing the lovely maiden in the hotel, and engaging rooms for the family (for here they intended remaining, temporarily, at least), and just had time to report to Gen. B— before noon.

The general in command had chosen a strong position, about ten miles south of the previous one; and hoped, by strongly fortifying himself, to be able to repel the enemy, and effectually check their advance. The erection of fortifications was vigorously commenced at once.

Though every hour in the day was fully occupied, Gen. B— found his brigade anxious enough to hear his second lecture, to assemble in the evening. They accordingly met, and heard a lecture, of which the following is a brief and imperfect synopsis.

The Second Lecture.—Our Duty to our Fellow-man.

"No one can be too well taught in relation to his duty to his fellow-man. If duty to self be perfectly understood, and acted out, one may be, perhaps, tolerably happy; for duty to self, in part, at least, affects our fellow-man. He who would be truly good and happy must look beyond self in the performance of duty. We should consider what those around us—those in daily communion with us, require at our hands. Certainly something must be done for their improvement, pleasure, or happiness; and each should ask himself, "What must I do?" And then, having learned his duty, press forward to its performance. Then:

1. Duty demands *kindness* toward those with whom we are connected. This is a proposition almost too plain for illustration or argument.

We have our companions around us—they eat, sleep, and live with us; and whatever of happiness we may be able to bring them, is required at our hands by *duty*. It is no indifferent matter to produce suffering, either mental or physical. *Unkindness* does produce mental suffering. Slights, jeers, and the like, though apparently little things, wound the sensitive heart. Then, if the one acting unkindly reflects upon his course, the stings of a wounded conscience continually prick him. Thus one unkind act may make two, or even more, unhappy. For the sake of *self*, then, as well as for others, *kindness* should characterise our intercourse with our fellow-beings.

2. Duty requires us to be *polite* to our companions, neighbors, and friends. Without politeness—that which is suggested by common sense, guided by a well-meaning heart—not senseless *etiquette*—man renders himself *disgusting*, rather than *pleasant*, to those around him. Impoliteness does not enter into pure hearts. Not to be consistently polite is, to a certain extent, to be unkind. It is more easy to treat those around us politely, than otherwise; for impoliteness often requires thought for its perfection, while its opposite arises naturally in the mind of the gentleman.

Again, to be knowingly impolite, we must overcome the reasoning of good sense, good nature, and a good heart.

True, a deadened state may be reached, in which the actors feels little or no compunction ; but such cease to be *gentlemen*—they are very near the brute creation, who can be habitually and intentionally impolite. They are below the level of sensibble men, and deserve only that treatment which is due to all enemeis of mankind at our hands. By being polite, we make others pleasant, remove some of the rough corners in our rugged life-path, and obtain for ourselves the regard of mankind.

3. Duty demands that we labor for the good and improvement of our companions.

Every man has something to do in life, and should seek his vocation, not only with reference to his own selfish preferences, but he should take into account the benefits to be conferred on others. If this rule were more nearly carried into effect, fewer clashes and jars would occur, and greater good result We should labor—

I. For the *moral* improvement of all—make every effort in our power to lift our fellow-men from the sinks of sin, and point them to the strait and narrow road that leads to the New Jerusalem.

O that all felt the importance of this ! Then would the gates of hell open less frequently to receive the eternally dying, while shouts of glad music would welcome the returned prodigals to a father's mansion. Happy he who is instrumental in saving one soul.

II. The *mental* improvement of those with whom we come in contact, should receive due consideration. Might we not, by a *word*, lead some one who now grovels in ignorance, to search the fields of wisdom? and thus render himself fit to enjoy more of the blessings so profusely lavished upon us? The unlettered child of ignorance knows but little of real enjoyment. His is rather a *negative* happiness (so to speak). cramped in narrow limits, he cannot soar into the fields of delight.

III. That we should attend to the physical comforts, or

good, of our companions, needs only to be hinted. Every one perceives the necessity of relieving physical suffering.

We come then:

4. To the consideration of duty towards our enemies, (for we all have enemies, even among our every-day associates). Many can point out those whom they know to be at enmity with them. Toward such, how shall we act?

Human nature says, "*Hate* for hate." But the more we hate an enemy, the wider the rupture becomes. Hatred never cures hatred; but, since "like produces like," new animosities spring up, new ruptures break forth, and, carried to an extreme, every man is at war with his brother.

Duty never suggested this mode of treatment; no, *never*. Our whole duty to our enemies is comprehended in the words, "*Love your enemies*." O it is *love* that softens the heart, cleanses it, makes it pure, and draws brother to brother in sweet communion! No enemy can long withstand the tender pleadings of this feeling.

Would we benefit our enemies, draw hatred from their hearts, and implant a holy feeling? Then let us love them, work for their good, break the chains that bind them, and make them worthy to be our friends, our companions, our own *loved* brothers. This is our duty to this class of men, as taught by God.

Then let us look to our hearts, and see that we cherish *love*. We need not love the sins of our enemies, but a desire for their *spiritual* welfare should be ever cherished for them.

Finally: We should *do unto others as we would that they should do unto us*. This includes our whole duty to man. We do not desire others to treat us badly, then we should not mistreat them. We want nothing but kindness, love, or honor from others; then we must give nothing else to them. How different would be the scenes of earth were every one to do as he would be done by. Quarreling, warring, and the like, would be at an end.

It is incumbent on every individual to do what he can
toward bringing about this happy end. Duty calls every
one to his post. Your own happiness, as well as that of
others, depends, in a great measure, upon the strict performance of duty to your fellow-man. Then, when so
much is at stake, it is but reasonable that every sensible
man should see to it, that the requirements of duty at his
hands, remain not unanswered."

The effect of this lecture could but result in good. Those
of the men who were engaged in petty quarrels and wrang-
lings, felt it as a direct rebuke to themselves; and many of
them resolved to do better in the future— to endeavor to
help their companions, instead of hindering them on every
occasion.

Gen. B— was much gratified during the next few days,
to notice the general feeling of friendship pervading his
men. Though there was hard work to do, and every one
had his allotted share, there was yet time to show kindness
to comrades.

Every day scouting parties were out, playing about the
lines of the enemy. Sometimes these parties were unfortunate enough to lose a man or two, either captured, killed,
or wounded; but in the aggregate we took more prisoners
than we lost.

The known ability of Virtus as a leader of scouting parties, often placed him in command. He found such labor,
though often beset with many dangers, preferable to working on the fortifications. It it needless to speak of his almost unparallelled success. One endowed with intellect and
caution, is not apt to be foiled or led astray by the wiles of
mere vassals.

A few days after the lecture last given, as the enemy
were still several miles away, and no immediate attack anticipated, Gen. B— determined to continue his course of
lectures. So, after the day's labor was finished, he called

his men together, and delivered a lecture, of which the following is a brief sketch :

" *Our Duty to our Country.*"

" I need offer no apology for again addressing you on the subject of *duty*, when it is remembered that he who knows, and performs every duty perfectly, is happy. An omission, or neglect of duty, causes unhappiness, so surely as the actor has not deadened his conscience, There is a state to which wickedness may lead man, where conscience loses the power to perform her office of *approval* or *reproval*. Those who arrive at this state feel no unhappiness at the commission of error or crime. They are dead to good works, and hence lose all appreciation for them; and so love wickedness that it appears *loveable* to them.

This may seem paradoxical to some; yet he who observes mankind cannot fail to admit its truthfulness.

Every relation in life calls forth its particular duties. There are duties peculiar to the family circle, to the church, to the community in which one lives, to mankind in general; but those duties of which I propose to speak, on the present occasion, have reference to one's country.

Then :

1. We must obey the laws of our country. We are all instrumental in making our laws; but few think much of the necessity of living in strict accordance with them. Our jails and penitentiaries teem with the violators of law. Look at the " motley crew," and decide whether their life is profitable to them. Lost to virtue, honor, integrity, they can but drift on through life, 'mid its vile filth and pollution. But not all violators enter prison walls. Many, whose hearts are 'rotten to the core,' evade the just decisions of the law. The land is full of such. Our jails are not large enough to hold them. And to this class belong the blackest villains ! This state of things is reached by refusing to comply with the behests of a righteous law.

Should all men become equally negligent, our laws might as well be abolished, and our country given up to irretrievable ruin.

When such is the case, what sensible man can say that *duty* requires nothing of him?

Would a people be united and happy? then let them obey the laws of their country. This they must do, if national prosperity is their object. A country divided against itself cannot stand; and where law is neglected, scisms and factions arise, opposed to each other.

Had those composing the old United States, observed simple *duty* in regard to their published laws, I have no hesitancy in saying that this bloody war would never have been instituted. See what desolation, then, neglect of duty to the laws of our country may bring about!

2. We must *fight* for our country. Every nation has its time of trouble—times when its citizens must gird themselves for the battle-field, or calmly rest while vandals forge chains for them, and then allow themselves to be led away captive. Shall another man rule me, the free-born? No. The love of freedom bids me cast off the chains, and meet the enemy face to face.

We can conceive of nothing that would justify one people in destroying another. As individuals, we are ever ready to defend ourselves against those who desire to injure us; and, bound together as a nation, the same feeling of self-defence prompts us to fight for the maintenance of our rights. Our country demands, and expects us to rescue her from the thraldom of the heartless invaders. Our mothers, sisters, wives, children—all expect us to save ourselves and them from the most disgraceful bondage. Hardships, privations, suffering, and danger, we must endure, for our country's good. He is not a patriot, who will murmur at any of the necessary hardships which his country's freedom requires him to make.

"More yet. The good of our country requires us to

keep ourselves free from all those evil habits which tarnish character, depreciate one's virtue, and make him unfit for the duties and responsibilities of dignified and useful citizenship.

" If all the liars, blackguards, whoremongers, gamblers, thieves, extortioners, blasphemers, demagogues—if all the base and corrupt characters in any country, were forced to leave it, that country would be much better, happier, and stronger, because of their removal.

" Virtue in the people is necessary to the well-being and prosperity of government, provided that government rests on virtue as its foundation. As, therefore, the vicious are a curse to the country, if we would be true patriots, we must be virtuous. To be virtuous, we must shun vice in whatever garb it presents itself."

Shortly after the beginning of the fortifications, the expected re-inforcements came up; making the entire command something more than half as great as the still advancing foe. But a few days elapsed before it became evident that the enemy intended attacking our men, so soon as they could prepare themselves.

Every precaution was taken to prevent surprises. Scouting parties were ever on the alert, and Virtus almost always out with them.

At times some of the brave scouters were captured; but they took more prisoners on an average than they lost.

When but a few miles lay between the opposing hosts, Gen. B— was commanded to make a "flank movement" with his brigade. This, his accurate knowledge of the country eminently fitted him to perform. While perfecting his hasty arrangements, he sent for Virtus, and said :

" This order is rather unexpected to me, and will cause me to disappoint my friend, Mr Love, whom I had promised to visit this evening on important business. Now, if you will oblige me by meeting him in my stead, you may

8

perhaps do so to your own interest, should you *happen* to see Miss Lula.

"If I am competent to transact your business, it will afford me much pleasure to do so. My regard for yourself would be a sufficient reason for my willingness, if there were no possibility of seeing an accomplished lady. But when the two are united, I can only say, General, I will be most happy to serve you," was the reply.

"Then I will unfold the business matters to you."

Duly instructed as to the matter of business, Virtus gladly set out for the hotel at ——. True, he might not, after all, see Miss Lula, but while there was a possibility of such a thing, his thoughts and feelings were kept buoyant.

He found Mr. Love awaiting the general, and after making known the reasons of his absence, the two proceeded at once to business. This was soon arranged to their mutual satisfaction. A very cordial invitation was extended to Virtus to remain to supper, which was loudly seconded by little Kate, who, seeking grandpa, happened to come in just then.

"O yes, Mr. Virtus, you must stay. Grandma and aunt Lula will both want to see you. Come on to the parlor now; we have just been wondering if you would ever come to see us again;" said she, in her merry, prattling way.

The opportunity was too good to be lost—so thought our hero, and consented to stay long enough at least to see into the parlor. So, lifting his cap, he gracefully entered the parlor, where he met a cordial welcome from Mrs. Morton and Miss Lula, who, grateful to him for his numerous acts of kindness, admired a soldier of such noble bearing, and a character in which were blended so many excellencies.

In this feeling both the ladies were agreed; but the whole truth, by a great deal, would not be told, to say that

Miss Lula did not entertain for him a different feeling, and one, too, of much higher order.

When, therefore, the noble Virtus entered the room, a thrill of love, and of almost sacred admiration sent the red life-fluid quick to her beautiful cheeks; while her black eyes were coruscant with the holy influence of unadulterated love. Nor would our hero have shown less signs of a kindred feeling within, had not a summer's sun and a soldier's hardships darkened and roughened the skin of the most cleanly warrior. It is not extravagant to say, that these young people *loved to love each other.*

The hero had been seated but a moment, when Mrs. Morton inquired if a battle was not imminent.

" Yes, Madam; before to-morrow's sun goes down, many a soldier will have gone to his long home !"

" How do you feel, sir, in view of the possibility of your being among that number?" inquired the motherly old woman.

" I hope, madam, that I am prepared for the *worst,* or rather, I would say, for the *best;* since I have committed myself into the hands of Him who assures me that 'all things work together for good to them that love the Lord.' Believing this precious promise, I know that every thing will be ordered for the *best.*"

" Then you do not fear to meet the invaders?"

" No, madam. God will take care of me.".

" Would to God," sighed the old lady, " that all our soldiers were willing to trust Him. Would that they all had an abiding sense of God's favor !"

" It would be a great consolation," modestly responded the hero, " if they were all Christians; for then, though the missiles of death should visit them, their souls would but enter the sooner upon the joys of Heaven. But," looking at his watch, and rising at the same time to his feet, " I must go—my brigade will be gone, or ready to move by the time I hasten back to camp."

"Can't you stay till supper? We would be delighted to have you do so if you can."

"Thank you, ladies; duty suggests that I hasten back to my command. I hope I will see you both again, if such be the will of Heaven."

"I hope so," responded each of the ladies; while tears collected in their eyes.

"If you are wounded; we will nurse you you," said Miss Lula, while love and sadness were beautifully blended in her countenance.

"Yes," interrupted the old lady, "you must order yourself directly to us—it will honor us to nurse so noble a soldier."

"I certainly feel very grateful for such friends," said Virtus; "and if I should be wounded I would deem it a great 'honor' to be nursed by you," glancing at both the ladies.

He then shook their hands and departed; the prayers, as well as the admiration of the ladies accompanying him.

Miss Lula's heart fluttered with anxiety for the welfare of him upon whom her affections were all centred. "O, that I may be so fortunate as to see him again!" she sighed as his manly form passed out of sight.

"I will do myself the justice," resolved our hero, "to disclose my feelings to this lady, if we ever meet again."

He soon arrived at camps and found his regiment ready to move. Snatching up his musket he hastily "fell in," an the brigade began to move.

The design of this move was to flank the enemy. and, if possible, destroy his wagon trains. To effect this, the brigade marched about four miles, through the woods, stopping but a short distance from the enemy's rear. Here they slept on the ground without blankets or fire.

About sunrise the next morning a heavy fire—artillery and then musketry—was heard in the direction of our fortifications. The engagement became general about 9 o'clock, a. m. But long before this Gen. B—, with his gallant band, had fallen upon the Yankee rains, destroying them in great numbers, and capturing many teamsters and stragglers. The enemy, hearing of the damage that he was doing them, sent a regiment of infantry and one battery, supposing that the movement in their rear was only a cavalry raid.

Apprised of their advance, he placed two of his regiments in ambush, near the road, to make complete work of the enemy. When the Yankee rear had passed the van of the party in ambush, a deliberate volley was poured into their ranks, causing many a vandal to bite the dust. Immediately after this a charge was made, and nearly every man, battery and all, was captured.

The work of destroying wagons was again resumed with great vigor; and another half hour found most of them in ruins.

Meantime the firing had been incessant in the front, indicating that the fiercest of battles was raging.

Learning the fate of the regiment and battery that had been sent to protect the wagons, the enemy now sent back a brigade of four regiments. Like their predecessors, these met a very similar fate. A deadly volley was received from the hill on the roadside, while the battery which had been captured, cut long lanes through their frantic columns! The enemy made no stand. Some fled to the woods on the other side of the road; others made their way, with great speed, back to the front; while many were captured.

It is proper to state that all that were captured were sent off into the woods, to prevent their recapture, should the enemy come back in great force.

Up to this time, Gen. B— had not lost one man.

Having destroyed the wagons the General ascended the ridge along which he had advanced the night before, and started in the direction of the front. He had not gone

more, perhaps, than three fourths of a mile, when he saw
that the enemy were retreating. Choosing a very strong
position which could not be flanked on but one side (on
the right), he resolved to meet the enemy, and do him all
the harm possible. Accordingly, his battery, which had
been sent along, was placed in position, and the troops were
strung all along the hill sides, protected by dense, heavy
timber.

When the Yankees approached within six hundred yards
of the batteay, it opened on them, while a most terrific fire
greeted them from the hill-top.

Pressed in front and rear, they became panic stricken,
and sought safety by retreating in wildest confusion, on the
side of the road where we had no forces.

Yet many—very many of them—were mowed down,
before they could reach the forest. The road was strewn
with their dead and wounded. Muskets and knapsacks
were scattered promiscuously wherever the flying foe had
passed.

It now became evident to Gen. B— that the enemy were
effecting their escape through the woods on the side of the
road opposite to the position occupied by his troops. He
accordingly moved his force, or two regiments of it to his
right, so as to intercept them, leaving the remainder of his
force to block up the road. This was indeed a dangerous
move, as there was a prospect of being run over by the stam-
peding Yankees; and should they "pluck up" courage
enough to fight, they might easily over-power him. But
he made the venture, throwing the two regiments right
into the path of the enemy. The enemy seeing his inferior force, prepared to charge over them; but this they
could not effect. The result was Gen. B— lost about 20
men; while the enemy had perhaps 100 killed and many
wounded. Now that our forces in the enemy's rear, were
pressing hard upon them, and they could not make their

escape in front, one division of the Yankee army surrendered

Still farther to Gen. B—'s right the vandals were making their escape ; as soon, therefore as the pr soners were properly cared for, he ordered his brigade up the road, at " double quick," with the view of obstructing the enemy's path. Nor was his effort in vain. He gained their front, causing another division, (or nearly so,) of the enemy to surrender.

Having as many prisoners as he could guard, it pained him that he was denied the pleasure of capturing more of the robbers. Able to do no more for the present, he marched the prisoners back to meet the commanding general, who, when they met him, was astonished to see the vast number of prisoners captured by one brigade.

Gen. B— reported to his superior officer the direction which the enemy had taken, and begged the privilege of pursuing them.

" We have done well enough for to-day," said the commander ; " let us make secure what we now have."

It was ascertained that our entire loss was 146 killed, and 372 wounded ; while that of the enemy was 1,200 killed, 2,500 wounded, and about 8,000 prisoners.

This was one of the most brilliant affairs of the war.

The yankees, by rapid marches, managed to effect their escape through the nearest gap in the mountain ; and Gen. B— marched back to the gap which he had formerly guarded. His gallant conduct made him a Major General.

It would be needless to say that Virtus did his whole duty in the great battle which resulted so disastrously to the yankees. The truth is, two of the most important movements made by Gen. B— in that memorable battle, were first suggested by our hero.

In Gen. B—'s account of the battle, the following language occurs :

" It affords me much pleasure to testify to the gallantry

of all the troops under my command. *Every one did his duty.* Great injustice, however, would be done, should I fail to mention the important service rendered me by private Virtus. The most important movements—those which resulted in the capture of the greater part of two divisions of the enemy—were made at his instance. Besides this, no soldier could have displayed greater daring and coolness than he exhibited during the entire engagement. This private is competent to be a major general. * * *"

When this report found its way into the papers, the praises of Virtus were on almost every tongue; and "the Authorities," through a friend, intimated that it would afford them pleasure to promote our hero, should his claims be formally presented.

When Gen. B— received the above information, he sent for Virtus to visit his head-quarters, and communicated to him the fact that he could receive an honorable appointment for his gallantry. When the hero heard this, he replied:

"I am gratified that I have been able to do my *duty*. The pleasure which arises from a consciousness of doing the best I could, is all the reward I claim. My *principles*, touching office, have not changed."

"It is needless," said the general, "for me to attempt to persuade you against your will; so I suppose I shall have to inform my correspondent that it is useless to confer office on you."

"I would prefer," said Virtus, "that you would use a little different phraseology, and say that you are *unable to answer my arguments;* for my position is based upon arguments which you have never answered."

"I accept the correction," said the general.

More of the present conversation cannot be narrated here. Gen. B—, however, wrote the following letter to his friend, in answer to his intimation that Virtus could receive an appointment:

'—— Gap, Aug. 1st, 1861.

Hon. —— — : Dear Sir, your favor of —— date has been received, and I hasten to reply.

" Private Virtus, whose intellect and attainments are not surpassed in the Southern States, whose moral principles, habits, and tastes, are more refined than those of any young man of my whole acquaintance, and whose military genius, coolness, and valor are, in my judgment, unsurpassed, if equalled, by those of any youth of his age—this young man, so well qualified to be a distinguished leader, utterly refuses all promotion. He sustains his refusal by numerous arguments, which no man in this division of the army can relute.

" Yet his services, though a private, cannot be easily estimated He is *the model* for every noble-minded soldier in my brigade; and already his influence is marked in my whole command. Besides, when we wish to find out the number and movements of the enemy—when any very dangerous or important expedition has to be made—*Private Virtus* is the man to whom is entrusted such business. We feel *proud* of him. The truth is, we could do better without the services of any other man in the division than without his; and I am not sure that the division would not suffer more by losing his services, than those of any officer connected with it. His influence extends to all grades— from the private to the general commanding. In a word, he is the *salt* of this division. His price is far above rubies.

* * * * *

Signed, B—.

Maj. Gen. Comm'g.

The enemy, it is needless to say, gained nothing by this invasion, save the loss of nearly two-thirds of their troops, all their wagons, &c., and the privilege of burning houses, stealing every thing they could carry with them, and insulting women.

When our brave soldiers settled down permanently at the

Gap, and had had time to rest themselves a little, our model chaplain, in the presence of a large audience, delivered a most thrilling sermon from the following text: " *The battle is not to the strong.*"

He said :

" It is in accordance with human philosophy that the heavier body should, when it meets a lighter one, repel it ; but, in the administration of human affairs, this is not always the case. ' The battle [i. e., the victory] is *not* to the strong,' as such, nor indeed to the weak : *God decides the fate of every battle.* To His interposition, we owe the recent great victory with which our armies have been crowned. Truly, ' He hath done great things for us, whereof we are (or should be) glad.'

" The present great war was brought upon us, not without a *cause.* God never punishes without a reason. Our people have sinned grievously against Him, and incurred His displeasure ; hence the present desolating war.

" It is clear to my mind that, if our people would remove the cause or causes of the war, God would bring the war to a speedy close. What are these causes ? and how can they be removed ? are questions of vital importance to our nation.

" The causes of the war are—

" 1. Political corruption—demagogues, base party leaders, an abuse of the elective franchise, rottenness in political parties. The people, generally, in giving their support to party rather than principle, sanctioned the corruption of their leaders, and thus virtue was driven from the government.

" 2. The individual wickedness of the people, in that they have refused to bow to the authority of Jesus, and have neglected His claims upon them—this has had much to do in bringing on the present war.

" 3. Religious corruptions and hypocricy—perverting the word of God, and making it subservent to worldly ends, assuming the garb of religion in which more successfully to serve *self* and the devil—these causes have had much influence in spreading the mantle of mourning over the country.

"If we would remove the present evils, we should first remove their causes. Will we do this? Let the people repent "in dust and ashes," of all their sins, and forsake them; then will God remove his chastening rod."

The discourse was well elaborated, the above being a mere synopsis. The sermon made a fine impression upon the minds of those who heard it; and many resolved that, so far as they were concerned, the causes of our troubles should be removed.

The next evening Gen. B— delivered a lecture on the following subject:

"*Our Duty to God.*"

Below are given the principal points of the discourse: .

1. We ought to obey His laws. But since the whole human family has fallen from His love and favor, and God has provided a way for our escape from hell, we should—

2. Believe in Christ Jesus, the Saviour of sinners. We should yield the most implicit obedience to every demand which He makes upon us. We should 'glorify Him in our bodies and spirits, which are His.'

3. We should 'walk in the Spirit.' He should be invited to take up his permanent abode in our hearts

4. We should love every body—enemies as well as friends—and do all in our power to benefit them.

5. The great objects of life should be to become as much like Christ as possible, and make as many good impressions as we can upon the minds of those with whom we associate."

This lecture, like all the others the general had delivered, made a fine impression. His men readily listened to every thing that fell from his lips.

It must not be supposed that Miss Lula failed to see the notice, in the papers, of our hero's conduct: yet, unlike too many women who would marry a man simply because he is an officer, she placed a light value on these newspaper puffs, except so far as the facts narrated in them tended to demonstrate the true nobility of him who, without apparent effort, had won her undivided affection. She, like the noble Virtus, thought little of " bars," " stars," and " wreaths"—intellectual and moral worth, in her estimation, were things of highest value.

She was greatly delighted to know that he passed through the battle unhurt; and secretly, yet modestly, sighed that she might see him once more.

Nor did the noble Virtus fail to think of the lovely Lula. " But *where* will she be ? When shall I see her again ?" were questions which, to a mind less disposed to confide every thing to the All-Wise, would have been productive of much anxiety. But Virtus had committed his interests —for time and eternity—into the hands of Him Who hath said, " All things work together for good to them that love Lord." In return for the confidence thus reposed, God gave him that comfort and composure of mind, which the world can neither give nor take away.

Those that honor God, God will honor. And so it proved in the present case. No man was ever more esteemed by his associates. All the good loved him; while the wicked seemed to stand in awe of him; though it was apparent that even they showed him great respect, at least outwardly. Then, again, Providence had brought him through many dangers. and had conferred more honor upon him in this way, than falls to the lot of many.

No hero of this or any other revolution ever exercised a more decided influence for good, or shared more liberally in their admiration and praises.

Gen B— was considered worthy of great respect, and this was every where awarded him; but Virtus' influence, though he was a mere private, was fully as extensive, and much more appreciated by the truly religious.

Honesty, strict integrity, and, above all, a living religion shone pre-eminently forth in the character of our brave hero. The mere mention of his name among those who knew him, was a most potent argument in favor of virtue, morality, patriotism, and religion. Whenever, therefore, any one in his regiment or brigade wished an elevated model of valor or piety, he would refer unhesitatingly to private Virtus.

Furthermore, it was evident that the noble character and bearing of our hero, and especially his elevation above office on reasons that the smartest generals had been unable to pull down, tended to make the privates content with and even proud of their position; while the distinction between privates and officers, in his division, at least, was through his influence, placed on its proper foundation, viz: *official*, not *intellectual* or *moral*. "A man's worth," said he, in conversation with an officer one day, "depends not upon the accidental circumstance of his being an *officer*; but if you would know what real worth is, you must look to a man's *moral* principles, his intellect; or if you desire to see the highest order of worth, you may find it in him who, besides having a polished intellect and correct moral principles, walks constantly with God. The importance of a man's existence may be estimated by the amount of pure moral and religious light reflected in his life. Regard man as a mirror, and God as the source of all pure and holy light; then is his life of most importance, who reflects most of this Heaven-born light. This is the correct principle on which to estimate a man's happiness. and, also, his usefulness. That man who reflects, in his life, nought but influences from the evil spirit, is a curse to himself, to his fellow-man, and to the world." Noble sentiments! worthy to be embalmed in every mind!

As soon as the general had a little leisure from his nume-

rous and pressing engagements, he invited Virtus to his
tent, where the following conversation took place:

"Did you see Mr. Love the evening before the battle?"
inquired the general.

"Yes, sir; and attended to the business you wished me
to."

"I am certainly much obliged to you.   Did you see the
fair Lula?"

"Yes, sir; I had the pleasure of a few mements' conversation with her?"

"Don't you want a furlough," laughingly inquired the
general, "to go down the road?"

"Thank you, general; while it would affords me pleasure
to go under other circumstances; it would be time ill spent
so long as my services are needed here.   When it becomes
certain that we will have a few weeks' leisure, I will not be
averse to being absent one or two days, though I have vowed never to ask for a furlough while the enemy desolate our
soil, and while I am able to do any thing towards driving
them back. But I don't know where your friend, Mr. Love,
or his family, will be, since their palatial residence has been
destroyed."

"I will find out, and let you know.   I will write to him
by the next mail."

"I am of opinion that the enemy will make no further
demonstrations in this part of the State, for several weeks;
hence a few days leave of absence for the purpose of *recre-
ation*, would be of advantage to you, and could do the
country no harm."

"Thank you, General, for all your kindness to me; but
I would rather, when I go, go under orders."

"That reminds me.   I wish to send some one to the
battle-field and vicinity to attend to some important business.   You are the very man!   Glad you mentioned it!
If you wish it I will detail you to start to-morrow."

"What is the character of the business? Pardon me for asking."

"I wish the effects of all my old regiment, who fell in the late battle, sent to their homes; and I must know how our wounded are getting on, (for you know they were left at hospitals near the battle-field)"

"Had you determined to send some one down there before the present conversation began?"

"I had not so determined, but I had thought of it as a thing desirable."

"I have a decided objection to going, unless you deem the business important. To have a plan fixed up for my accommodation merely, is what, in the name of patriotism, virtue and religion, I would most earnestly protest against."

"I intend, not for your accommodation merely, but especially because it is humane to do so, to look after the effects of our dead friends, and see how the wounded are doing."

"All I wished was that if I went on business it might be important business. While it would afford me much pleasure, ordinarily, to visit my friends, and enjoy some relaxation from hardships, I know I should be much dissatisfied, even in the presence of those whom I esteem most highly, should I be absent from the post of duty; yet if duty calls me where those friends are, I would most gladly call to see them."

After Virtus closed the above remarks there was a pause for a few moments, during which time some such thoughts as these passed through the General's mind:

"Noblest of the noble! Here is a Southern youth in whom there is not the least shadow of guile! I would rather possess his intelligence, his moral principles, and his living faith—in fine, I would rather be *private Virtus* than to be King of earth. He is one whom God delights to honor. A better rounded character I have never seen. If the walls of the New Jerusalem are built up with the most precious stones, his character is made of the most excellent principles, graces and proprieties. If 'An honest man is the noblest work of God,' then should this youth be esteemed among the noblest, if not the *noblest* of the *noble.*"

At length the General broke the silence by saying: "I fully appreciate your principles. You would be glad for *duty* to lead you to the place where Miss Lula is, yet, much as you would be delighted to see her, you are unwilling to absent yourself from the army on a flimsy pretext. This reveals to me the important fact, viz: that *duty* in your case, is stronger even than *love;* while the reverse is true as a general rule.

"Now, my dear sir, the disclosure of this fact elevates you more in my estimation than if you had performed one of the grandest feats known to chivalry. Yet I must send some one to attend to these matters, previously mentioned, and to attend to other busines of importance; and I know of no one to whom I could entrust them so well as to yourself. If you object to going on this basis, there is only one other way in which it is possible for you to go."

" What 'way' is that?" inquired Virtus.

" I shall have to detail you, with your consent Of course, I will not send you *without* your consent."

" Then make the detail, and I am ready to be gone."

www.ingramcontent.com/pod-product-compliance
Lightning Source LLC
Chambersburg PA
CBHW032011010726
47493CB00007B/2354